Hearts **racing.**
Blood **pumping.**
Pulses **accelerating.**

Falling in love can be a blur... especially at 180 mph!

So if you crave the thrill of the chase—on and off the track—you'll love

NO TIME TO LOSE
by Carrie Weaver!

"No offense, Ms. Tanner, but it takes more than an engineering degree to troubleshoot a performance engine."

"None taken. I've been around the shop since I learned to walk. My dad taught me everything he knows. I'll do my part to make sure that engine is in perfect running condition. My father would never let a substandard motor out our doors."

"Maybe not intentionally. But I've turned a few wrenches myself and I can tell you it's in the engine. You just concentrate on diagnosing the problem. The motor needs to be shipshape for qualifying Friday."

"I'll see that it is."

Hopefully, she would rise to the challenge. Because failure wasn't an option. His whole career was on the line.

Dear Reader,

The other day, my two teenage sons came home from a visit at their father's house. Their roughhousing started almost immediately and I warned, "Shh, it's the last five laps of the race."

They rolled their eyes and told me I was becoming just like their dad. Which was a compliment of sorts, because their dad remains a good guy trying to be the best parent he can. He was and is an avid NASCAR fan and introduced me to the sport early in our relationship.

Like lots of folks who have been through a divorce, I had lonely times when the silence seemed so hollow it made my heart ache. I'd turn on the TV to fill the silence. And, surprisingly, I found tuning in to NASCAR reassuring. Surprising because NASCAR had been my ex-husband's passion and I'd simply been along for the ride. Or so I'd thought. But I found myself getting caught up in the race every time I passed the television. Gradually I chose my own favorite drivers—not just the drivers we'd chosen as a family.

When my Harlequin Superromance editor, Laura Shin, asked if I might be interested in writing a romance involving NASCAR racing, my response was a resounding "Yes!" She expressed my sentiments to Marsha Zinberg, who ultimately asked me to participate in Harlequin's officially licensed NASCAR series. *No Time To Lose* is my first book in the series, and I sincerely hope you enjoy it!

Yours in reading,

Carrie Weaver

P.S. I enjoy hearing from readers and can be contacted by e-mail at CarrieAuthor@aol.com, or snail mail at P.O. Box 6045, Chandler, Arizona 85246-6045.

NASCAR®

NO TIME TO LOSE

Carrie Weaver

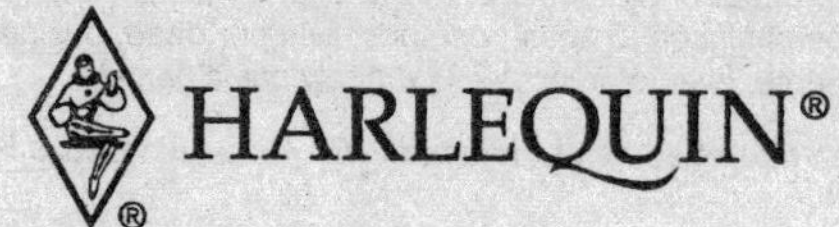

TORONTO • NEW YORK • LONDON
AMSTERDAM • PARIS • SYDNEY • HAMBURG
STOCKHOLM • ATHENS • TOKYO • MILAN • MADRID
PRAGUE • WARSAW • BUDAPEST • AUCKLAND

ISBN-13: 978-0-373-21772-4
ISBN-10: 0-373-21772-2

NO TIME TO LOSE

Carrie Weaver is acknowledged as the author of this work.

This edition published by arrangement with Harlequin Books S.A.

www.eHarlequin.com

Printed in U.S.A.

CARRIE WEAVER

With two teenage sons, two dogs and three cats, Carrie Weaver often feels she lives in a state of choreographed chaos. Her books reflect real life and real love, with all the ups, downs and emotion involved.

This book is for Bobby.
Thanks for sharing so many good times over the years and being an active father to our sons.

ACKNOWLEDGMENTS

Special thanks to Laura Shin, Marsha Zinberg and Tina Colombo at Harlequin Books. This book wouldn't have happened without you. And to Catherine McNeill at NASCAR for providing the technical expertise I lack. Any errors are mine.

CHAPTER ONE

JAMIE shook off a wave of regret as she pulled into the parking lot at McGuireville Community Hospital. She found a space and parked the rental Mustang—red, of course.

Please have him be okay.

Resting her forehead on the steering wheel, she allowed herself a moment of weakness. What would she do if he died? The world without Jimmy Tanner was too scary to contemplate, even though he'd let her down all those years ago. Somehow, she'd always felt the world would continue to rotate on its axis as long as her daddy was in the engine-building shop. Maybe because that meant there was still a chance for things to turn out right.

Jamie straightened, reaching for her Detroit Pistons ball cap as she flipped down the vanity mirror on the visor. She smoothed her hair into a ponytail and twisted an elastic band to hold it, then pulled the tail through the back of her cap. She settled the brim low on her forehead. There. No one would remember her as a Poultry Princess now. And her mom wouldn't think she'd succeeded in molding her only daughter into a proper Southern lady.

She pressed the lock tab for the Mustang and hurried to the double doors. Raising her chin, she prepared for what was to come. A burly guy did a double take as she walked by then let out a low whistle.

Jamie ignored him. Glancing down, she realized her scoop neck T-shirt fit more snugly than she realized. Her clothes were normally chosen with care, sure to deflect rather than draw attention.

Jamie shrugged. Nothing to be done about it now. When she reached the information desk, the volunteer seemed familiar.

"Why, Jamie Lynn Tanner, I haven't seen you in ages. Not since the Poultry Princess pageant."

Jamie managed a smile. "I'm here to see my father. Is my mother already with him?"

"Yes, dear. The waiting room is on the second floor, to the right. Tom's upstairs, too."

"Of course. Thank you, Mrs. White." Luckily, she'd remembered the woman's name.

"Certainly, dear. Your mother will be so pleased you're home. I'm sure she'll have you back wearing a dress in no time," she said, smiling.

Jamie suppressed a groan. That's what she was afraid of.

Choosing the stairs, she took them two at a time to make herself feel strong and in control. Because if there was one thing she felt around her family, it was out of control.

TOM TANNER GLANCED up from his cup of machine-dispensed coffee and stiffened. His sister, ubermechanic extraordinaire and their father's favorite, strode across the lobby to the waiting area. This was when he generally faded into the woodwork. But not now.

His mother patted his arm. "Be nice," she warned.

"I will if she will."

"That's not what I asked. I want you to be the bigger person and make her feel welcome."

Yeah, when hell freezes over. "I'll try," he murmured, ashamed at his knee-jerk competitive reaction. He had a hard time remembering the days when he'd thought his big sister hung the moon and the stars.

His mother rose, enfolding Jamie in a hug. "You made it." Her voice contained a note of relief, as if by Jamie's mere presence, she could heal her father.

"I'm sorry my flight was cancelled last night. I caught the first plane I could." Jamie pulled from her mother's embrace. Nodding in his direction, she said, "Tommy."

The diminutive nickname from his childhood rubbed him the wrong way. He responded in kind. "Hi, Metal Mouth."

Amusement lurked in her green eyes, so much like their mother's. "Thanks, Boy Wonder." It was a backhanded reference to his childhood obsession with superheroes.

Tom slouched in his seat. Why did he feel like a gawky kid again? The answer stood before him in all her blonde perfection. Even in casual clothes and a ball cap, Jamie was clearly blessed with the good looks in the family. No wonder there hadn't been many left over for him.

"No problem, Your Highness," he said.

His sister flushed. Score one for the kid brother.

"Stop it you two," their mother scolded.

Shrugging off his irritation, he allowed himself to be the bigger person, as his mother had put it. His voice was husky when he said, "It's good to see you, Sis."

And, surprisingly enough, it *was* good to have her back. He just didn't want her staying too long.

Jamie smiled, showing off her excellent orthodontia. She leaned down and hugged him quickly. "Hey, Tom. It's good to see you, too."

He swallowed hard. Losing his sister had been wrenching. But having her back could destroy everything he'd worked for.

She straightened, addressing their mother. "How's Daddy doing?"

"They already have him up and around if you can believe it. I thought it was too soon after a quadruple bypass, but they start rehabilitation right away."

"Probably for the best. You know Dad—he doesn't like to sit around much," Tom commented.

His mother straightened. "He's going to be taking it a lot easier. Isn't he, Tom?"

Tom would have preferred to face a pack of angry stock car drivers than face his mom when she'd made a decision. He knew when to admit defeat. If only temporarily. "Yes, ma'am."

"Jamie, the doctor should be done examining your father if you'd like to see him. We'll wait here. Your brother has a business proposition to discuss with you after that."

"*Mom.*" Even he detected a whine in his voice. Here he was, a grown man and partner in a world-renowned performance engine business, and he was reduced to sniveling. He shot his sister a look.

"Thomas Edward Tanner."

That was all it took. Tom sighed. "Yes, ma'am. Jamie, I'll talk to you over lunch."

Jamie nodded, frowning.

Tom watched her ponytail swing in time with her confident stride. He had the feeling Cyclone Jamie was about to unleash her damage and it would be his career that took the hit.

JAMIE TIPTOED into her father's room. His eyes were closed and he was hooked up to all sorts of machines. She sat in the chair next to the bed, taking the opportunity to watch him, really noticing how much he'd aged in recent years.

His hair was mostly gray and his face rounder, yet more lined. Her heart ached at the changes in him. And for the fact that she'd been away so much during the last twelve years.

As if sensing her gaze, her father opened his eyes. "Jamie," he murmured.

She grasped his hand. "I'm here, Daddy."

"Yes, you are." He tried to smile, but it was a pale version of his usual cocky grin.

"You scared me."

"I scared myself. I'm glad you came. Your mother needs someone to lean on...I worry about her."

"Daddy, she's one of the strongest people I know. But I'll do what I can. You just concentrate on getting well."

"The old ticker's good as new. Maybe even better."

"You just had a quadruple bypass. That's serious stuff. I'm sure your doctor is going to expect you to make some lifestyle changes."

He grimaced. "Yeah, a social worker's going to talk to us about that. And a nutritionist. Your mother's already talking about getting a bunch of heart-healthy cookbooks."

"Good for her. She'll keep you on the straight and narrow."

"You know it." He rubbed her hand with his thumb. "It's good to see you, Kitten."

Her throat constricted at his use of his old pet name. "Yeah. Good to see you, too."

I've missed you, Daddy. But she couldn't bring herself to say the words. Instead, she opted for a quick retreat to regroup. "I'm gonna let you rest. I'll be back later this afternoon."

He nodded. His lack of protest bothered her. He was weaker than he would admit.

JAMIE PUSHED the lettuce around with her fork. She eyed Tom. His appetite seemed unimpaired.

"How's your chicken fried steak?" she asked.

"Excellent, as usual. The diner has the best food this side of Mom's table."

"Their salads could use some imagination."

"We have simple tastes here in Arkansas. You've gotten spoiled in the big city." His smirk told her he thought she'd always been treated specially.

She decided not to rise to her brother's bait. "Hmm. We best not debate who's more spoiled or we could be here for days. Dad's concerned about Mom having our support. It won't help if we're at each other's throats all the time."

Tom sighed. "Yeah. Mom's worried about Dad and

Dad's worried about Mom. And we're stuck in the middle."

"We're their kids. That's where we're supposed to be. Besides, I think it's kind of cute."

Tom snorted.

"I take it you don't have anyone special to worry over you like that? Things didn't work out with Tiffany or Brittany or whatever her name was?" she asked.

"Nope. I'm married to my job. How about you?"

"The same." Except that her job would be nonexistent in a couple of months. Who knew sales of domestic minivans could take such a hit?

"I thought things were going to work out with you and that engineer."

"I thought so, too." Her words were quiet, her hurt probably evident. It still stung to think she'd actually believed they'd had a shot at the white picket fence and two-point-five kids.

Jamie shrugged to defuse her vulnerability. "He couldn't figure out why I need to spend so much time helping out at the racetrack when I design engines all day. It's an outlet that keeps me sane, allows me to be hands-on in a way I can't be at work."

"And his outlet?"

"Getting hands-on with a sweet young thing from the accounting department."

"Ouch." Tom winced.

"It was almost a year ago. I'm over it."

"Sure. He didn't deserve you anyway."

Jamie hoped she didn't detect a trace of pity in his voice. She sipped her sweet tea, stalling for time. Finally, she phrased a question that nagged at her. "How is it that our parents, who have such a strong marriage, could produce two children who can't seem to get relationships right?"

"Hey, I didn't say I couldn't get it right. I just don't want to at the moment. My career's too important."

"Yeah, you're a horrible liar, *Tommy*. Always were." She was gratified to see the tips of his ears redden. They were back on solid, familiar ground.

"And you're a sanctimonious bi—"

She raised her hand, palm outward. "Ah-ah. You wouldn't want me to tell mom you're being uncooperative, would you?"

He slouched in the booth, his glum expression so reminiscent of when he'd been a kid it almost tugged at her heart. Almost.

"D'you ever notice we both turn into ten-year-olds when we're together?" she asked.

"You mean you're not that way all the time?" His eyes sparkled with amusement.

"Let's make a real effort to act like adults. What's the business proposition Mom mentioned?"

"Promise you'll hear me out?"

"Sounds like you already know I'm not going to like it."

"I've brought in a lot of new business lately. Tanner has never been busier and Dad's going to be recuperating for a few months. Or retiring completely if Mom has her way."

"No way. Dad will never retire."

"No, I don't think so, either. But this heart attack shook him up. And we have to cover for him for at least six months."

"So what's that got to do with me?" Jamie tried to keep her expression bland. But she held her breath all the same.

"Mom said something about your Michigan division shutting down. She thought you, um, might consider coming back for a while."

Jamie raised an eyebrow. Her mother had always opposed her daughter working in the shop. That's why she left Arkansas in the first place.

"Under what terms?"

"Same terms that Dad offered when you graduated from college. I'll oversee the technical areas, you'll take some of the administrative stuff off my hands. And I'll build engines till Dad's back on his feet."

No wonder her mother hadn't objected. It was the same crummy deal she'd been offered before—designed to keep her pushing papers and away from engine-building.

Jamie wadded up her napkin and threw it on the table. "Thanks, but no thanks." She started to rise, but Tom grasped her arm.

"Wait. Can't we talk about this? Compromise?"

"So far I haven't heard any compromise. I made it clear twelve years ago that I had no intention of being a glorified secretary with an engineering degree. I'm certainly not going to be your secretary now."

"Administrative assistant."

"Whatever. Don't go politically correct with me, Tom. It doesn't suit you."

"It's a management position. We'll pay whatever you're making as an engineer. Or more."

Jamie shook off his hand. "Money's not the issue and

we both know it. I want complete control of the shop. Nothing less. *You* can keep the administrative stuff."

"No way. You're just as bullheaded as you've always been. Think of someone other than yourself. Dad needs you. Do it for him."

"Nice try." She ignored a pang of remorse, determined he wouldn't use her emotions against her. "Family guilt doesn't work on me anymore."

Tom's eyes narrowed. "Okay. I'm willing to give you the run of the shop for six months—under my supervision."

"Don't do me any favors. I'll stay at the house until Dad's out of the hospital, then I'm heading back to Michigan."

"To do what? Take a pay cut and transfer to another area?"

"I have other options."

"But not like this." He leaned forward. "Building performance motors, not those pansy passenger machines that the big automakers like to call engines. We're talking power, speed and *challenge*. I've never known you to back away from a challenge. And, hey, if that's not enough, this is your chance to prove you're the best engine-builder Tanner Performance Motors has ever seen."

Oh, boy, did her brother know which buttons to push.

"And what if I say yes?"

"We'll go to contract."

She eyed him, trying to decipher his motive. "Why do you suddenly want me back at Tanner? I've always thought you were happy being Dad's right-hand man."

He sipped his drink. "Look, it's not my idea. It's Mom's. But I'm gonna sink fast if I don't get help. We're way too busy to be down a man. Especially since it's Dad."

Nodding, she commented, "He always did the work of two."

"Or three. Come on, Jamie, you know you want this."

Yes, God help her, she *did* want it. She just wasn't sure she could handle another family betrayal.

"I wasn't good enough for the family business twelve years ago, but now I am—because you're caught between a rock and a hard place? Why should I put myself in that position again?"

"Because we're family. And in her own weird way, maybe Mom's trying to right a wrong, but she's too proud to come out and apologize."

Jamie swallowed hard. She wanted to believe him. All she'd ever wanted was to be accepted as a topnotch engine-builder and an important part of the family business. Her mother thought the shop was no place for a proper lady. "I'll think about it."

"Don't think too long. If you don't accept, I'll have to find someone else right away." His gaze was hard. Somewhere along the line, her baby brother had grown into a determined man.

"You know, a week ago I would have told you where you could put that offer." She glanced away. "Daddy's heart attack was a wake-up call. I don't want regrets if something happens to him."

"Exactly."

Taking a deep breath, she said, "Okay. I'll do it."

He nodded. "Good. Did I mention I had a contract drawn just in case?" He pulled a sheaf of papers from his briefcase and slid them across the table.

She stiffened. "No, you didn't."

"I'm sure you'll want to look over the terms." Tom's tone was casual. Too casual. "There's a twenty-four hour bail-out clause, so you can sign now and have time to review the fine print."

"I can see that." She scanned the pages. "Hey, what's this about handling customer relations as needed?"

"You know there's hand-holding that goes with the territory. When a crew chief orders a high-dollar engine, he expects immediate feedback."

"I remember Dad taking calls at all hours." She also remembered the interrupted suppers and missed school programs. Being single had its advantages at times. "I can do the hand-holding. Let me skim the rest of the document."

"Sure, no pressure."

Yeah, right.

Jamie read the remainder of the contract. It was simple and straightforward. She signed both copies, handing them back to her brother.

He signed and dated, giving her a copy.

"When do I start?"

"Tomorrow morning."

Raising an eyebrow, she commented, "You don't waste any time."

"We don't have any time to lose." He removed a manilla envelope from his briefcase. "Besides, your flight for Phoenix leaves at six o'clock tomorrow morning."

"Huh?" Jamie figured jet lag had addled her brain or scrambled her hearing. "What's in Phoenix?"

"The Pearce Racing Team. Ryan Pearce is running

one of our engines in the Number 63 car Saturday night. That's NASCAR NEXTEL Cup Series."

"I know darn well what it is. NASCAR is nearly my religion."

"Good. Because Pearce is hotter than hell and his people can't seem to figure out what's wrong with the engine. He was a mechanic in his pre-racing days and swears it's mechanical."

Jamie snorted. "Pearce just can't run with the big boys. He got lucky in the Busch Series, but now that he has some real power under him, he can't handle the pressure."

"Probably. But we've still got to check it out." He placed a plastic sack on the table. "You'll need these, too."

"What is it?" She opened the bag and removed a Kelly-green T-shirt with a small Tanner logo on the front and a matching baseball cap.

"You'll wear the Tanner T-shirt when you're at the track."

"Didn't they have a larger size? It looks a little small."

"Nope." Tom's right eye twitched, a sure sign he was lying. "And lose the Pistons hat. We're a good, Southern-based, family-owned and operated company. No Yankee paraphernalia."

"Like it matters what I wear."

"Oh, it matters. I figure we might get some prime national coverage. You can't buy that kind of PR."

Jamie straightened. "I intend to build the best product available and keep our customers happy. I don't care about camera time."

"Humor me, okay?" Tom took the T-shirt from her

hands and turned it over. Tanner Performance Motors was emblazoned on the back, the lettering so large it almost bled onto the sleeves.

"Subtle, Tom, subtle. They could see this from the blimp."

"That's the idea. And look on the bright side—at least the shirt doesn't say Poultry Princess." His smirk made her blood boil.

Jamie leaned back, crossing her arms. "Tom, you can make all the digs you want about the pageant, but it's not going to change a thing. That title shows I can do anything I set my mind to—even if it was Mom's idea. Barring Daddy, I was the best engine-tech at Tanner Motors twelve years ago and I'm still the best. And I intend to stick around and prove it."

CHAPTER TWO

RYAN PEARCE GLANCED at the tachometer and hammered the throttle. He swore under his breath. The response was sluggish, even when he geared down. How was he to win the race with this hunk of junk? The D-shaped Phoenix track required speed in the dogleg and there was no room for error in the turns.

He pulled into the pit and hauled himself out of the window. His crew chief, Trey Walker, shook his head. "You're hesitating again."

"I'm *not* hesitating. It's the damn car."

"When's the rep from Tanner supposed to get here?"

"Tom Tanner said he'd send an engineer first thing this morning." He glanced at his watch. "It's nearly noon. He'd better not be yanking my chain."

"Come on, Ryan, I'm sure he's not messing with you. I heard his dad's sidelined with a heart attack."

Ryan swiped his hand over his face. "Yeah. One of my phone calls caught Tom as he was leaving the hospital. I was, um, a little pushy, considering his family situation. I couldn't help it. My career is at stake. I'm taking control of this situation."

"I'm sure he understood. You've got a lot riding on this race. And if he's sending an engineer, that means he's taking the problem seriously. Who's coming from Tanner?"

"Some whiz with a degree from Georgia Tech who, quote, 'knows engines better than anyone else.'"

"This whiz got a name?"

"Jamie. He didn't give a last name and I was too ticked off to ask."

"Jamie Tanner, the hottie?" Trey smirked.

Ryan started to simmer. "What do you mean?"

"Years ago the Tanner family was featured in a magazine—I can't remember which one—as one of the engine-building companies on the rise. She was one good-looking woman. And if I remember correctly, I read she went to Georgia Tech. Probably a cheerleading scholarship or something."

Swearing under his breath, Ryan wanted to put his fist through a wall. Or Tom Tanner's face. "I'm tired of people treating me like some guy from the sticks who couldn't tell a carburetor from my elbow. Is this some kind of joke?"

"I assure you, Mr. Pearce, I'm no joke." A blonde woman in a Pistons hat and a faded Georgia Tech T-shirt pushed away from the wall. She extended her hand. "I'm Jamie Tanner."

He eyed her hand before taking it. She had a firm grip, but not overly aggressive. He didn't like women who tried to prove they could arm wrestle a guy to the ground. "Ryan Pearce. You're here to troubleshoot?"

"Yes. My brother Tom wanted to make sure this situation was handled immediately. I understand your concern."

"No offense, Ms. Tanner, but it takes more than an

engineering degree to troubleshoot a performance engine."

"None taken. I've been around the shop since I learned to walk. My dad taught me everything he knows."

"Jimmy Tanner has a topnotch reputation. That's why I chose Tanner Motors. I didn't want to get lost in the shuffle with a big supplier. And my team owner didn't see the need to hire an engine-builder. Maybe with a few wins under my belt, that will change."

"I'll do my part to make sure your engine is in perfect running condition. My father would never let a substandard motor out our doors."

"Maybe not intentionally. But I've turned a few wrenches myself and I can tell you it's in the engine."

Jamie's eyes narrowed and she inclined her head. "I'll take that into consideration. My specialty tools will be shipped if I need them. I brought a few basics in my luggage. May I borrow your tools in the meantime?"

Ryan glanced at the black duffel bag slung over her shoulder, noting the manufacturer's name. Sure, she carried high quality tools, but that could be window dressing. "I'm very particular about my tools."

"So am I." Her gaze was level. He found her intensity reassuring.

"You'll have full access to the equipment in the track shop. But don't touch anything in the hauler or on the pit cart without asking."

Her mouth tightened. "I wouldn't dream of it."

"Good. We understand each other."

JAMIE BIT HER TONGUE, careful not to tell him what he could do with his understanding. Ryan Pearce had a chip on his shoulder and she had to tread carefully. From what she'd overheard, his crew chief hadn't got very far suggesting the problem was with Pearce's driving. The suggestion would be even less welcome from her.

It looked like he'd hesitated in the turn. A rookie mistake. Pearce had been fairly impressive in the NASCAR Busch series, but there was a heck of a lot of added pressure in the NASCAR NEXTEL Cup series.

"Come on. I'll take you to the hauler first, then the shop," he offered. "My crew chief will be busy tabulating the numbers on my run. Won't he?" Pearce glared at Trey.

Trey didn't seem intimidated. He shrugged and ambled off, whistling under his breath.

His insouciance didn't seem to bother Pearce. Instead, it made him grin. "Best crew chief in the business or I wouldn't stand for his crap."

"He's got quite a reputation." Not all of it good.

Pearce shrugged. "I don't pay much attention to track gossip. I judge my friends by their actions. My enemies, too."

His words made her uneasy. She'd heard he was desperate for a win. Desperate men had no business driving one hundred and eighty miles an hour with forty-two other cars. They were a danger to themselves and to others. "Do you have many of those? Enemies?"

"A few."

"Think anyone's been tampering with your car?"

"I'm not with the car 24/7, but I trust my crew. It's your job to find out what the problem is."

Great. He'd already made up his mind it was Tanner

Motors' fault. Jamie would accept the blame if it proved to be true. But there were an awful lot of variables to consider first.

They reached the row of team haulers. He took her to the blue and silver hauler emblazoned with his sponsor's logo. Two crew members stood under the awning, debating whether suspension or tires would be more crucial to a win at the Phoenix track. He introduced them to Jamie.

The aroma of meat roasting on the gas grill should have been enticing—she'd had very little breakfast—but Jamie's stomach was knotted with anticipation.

"Let's go inside."

She followed Pearce into the lounge. With upholstered benches, padded chairs and a big-screen TV, it was plusher than the great room in Jamie's Michigan condo.

"Help yourself to anything in the fridge. My driver keeps it well stocked."

"Thanks."

He removed a bottled water and twisted the cap. "Want one?"

"No, I'm good."

"Where are you staying?"

"I'm booked at a hotel nearby, but I don't figure I'll be spending much time there. A place to shower, mostly."

He nodded, his frown easing. "I hoped you didn't expect luxury. Track life isn't what most people think."

Impatience tugged at her. "I've been around tracks all my life, Mr. Pearce. There's not a whole lot that will surprise me."

"Call me Ryan. Working is different than visiting the pits."

"I've worked alongside my dad in the pits, too. He does whatever's necessary to ensure satisfaction with our motors. I intend to do the same."

"I hope so. I'll show you the equipment storage and work area." He led her down a short hallway with cabinets on either side. "Here's a workbench you can use for small stuff. I imagine you'll be in the track garage most of the time, though."

"Mmm-hmm."

"Again, you need any equipment from here, talk to me or Trey. We're running short-handed. My car chief, Bill, had some unexpected family business in Charlotte. He'll be here later."

"Who's been working on this engine? Bill?"

"Yeah."

Jamie filed away that piece of information. "Good. The fewer people messing with it, the better."

"Like I said, I trust my crew. You just concentrate on diagnosing the problem. The motor needs to be shipshape for qualifying on Friday."

She resisted the urge to roll her eyes. She was well aware how important qualifying was. "I'll see that it is."

"I'll show you the shop." They backtracked and stepped outside.

She replaced her hat, pulling the brim low to offset the harsh glare of the Arizona sun. Acutely aware of Ryan's presence, Jamie wished she was better at small talk.

He didn't jump in to fill the void. A few moments later, he said, "Here's the shop."

Jamie stepped into the garage, her eyes adjusting after the bright sunlight. The Number 63 car had already been brought over.

"You'll want the motor in the car for diagnosis?" he asked.

She nodded. "Yes. I might remove it later, depending on what I find."

"The hoist's over there. Yell if you need help."

"Thanks, but it won't be necessary. I can manage on my own."

He held her gaze for a moment. Nodding, he said, "Okay, I'll leave you to it. I need to see how Trey's coming with those stats."

Jamie breathed a sigh of relief when he left. The aroma of motor oil and solvent never failed to calm her senses. She removed her hat, then replaced it with the brim backward so it wouldn't block the light when she inspected the engine.

It seemed like only moments later when Jamie became aware of someone next to her. She glanced up to find Ryan inches away.

He leaned over the engine. "Didn't want to startle you. You seemed pretty intent."

Jamie wiped her face on the sleeve of her T-shirt. Sweat stung her eyes. "I get that way when I'm working. It used to frustrate the heck out of my mom. She claimed I ignored her calling, but I wouldn't have heard a bomb if it exploded next to me."

Grinning, he said, "Yeah, I had pretty much the same experience. My mom used to say it was selective hearing."

"My daddy always understood, though, so he'd talk Mom out of punishing me."

His grin faded. "What did you find?"

"None of the diagnostics turned up anything unusual. I'm not hearing a miss or a hesitation."

"I can't hear anything, either. But it's there."

"I've tried it under load. Sharp acceleration. Slow acceleration. Nothing."

"Slow acceleration isn't a problem, believe me."

Jamie tried to give him the benefit of the doubt. "It's a diagnostic clue, though."

"I guess. Like I said, it's intermittent. I haven't detected a pattern. What do you plan next?"

"I'll pull the motor, do a partial tear down and a visual inspection."

"Sounds reasonable."

"That surprises you?" Irritation and fatigue gave her words an edge she instantly regretted. "I'm sorry. This project is very important to me."

"I'm glad to hear that. Now, I'm also pretty sure I hear your stomach growling. A race car needs fuel to run and so do you. Come on, there are burgers on the grill. Unless, of course, you're a vegetarian?"

She chuckled, suddenly aware of her hunger. "No daughter of Jimmy Tanner could be vegetarian. I'll take mine rare, with lots of onions."

"A woman after my own heart."

RYAN EYED JAMIE as he swigged his cola. She had the appetite of a truck driver—her burger disappeared in record time. A small bag of chips soon followed. And now, she was eyeing his plate.

He couldn't help but smile. "There are a couple more on the grill. Help yourself."

She blushed. "When I'm working, I eat when I get the chance. It might be sixteen hours before I eat again so I think I'll take you up on seconds."

She headed outside to the grill. He'd have to be subhuman not to notice how nicely her jeans fit.

Uh-uh. None of that. *Focus, Pearce.*

Trey came in carrying a plate. He grabbed a soda and sat in one of the easy chairs. "I can't believe it's only April and nearly a hundred degrees out there. You're going to sweat your rear off during the race, Ryan."

"No kidding. It's a dry heat, though. Or so they say."

Jamie returned and sat down. "You keep dry ice in your ventilation system?"

"Yeah. The interior will top one-twenty this weekend, I'm sure."

"I don't know how you guys stand it. Four hours sitting in a moving oven. They'd have to pour me out of my uniform."

"Sometimes it feels that way. I dropped ten pounds at Daytona."

Trey stood and approached the table. He extended his hand. "Allow me to properly introduce myself. I'm Trey Walker, crew chief."

Jamie wiped her hand on a napkin and shook hands. "I'm Jamie Tanner. Do I detect a trace of Arkansas?"

She smiled, a gesture that made Ryan pause. Jamie Tanner was one beautiful gearhead when she smiled. But beautiful women and serious racing didn't mix—too many distractions, too much room for error.

"Yep. I grew up in Batesville." Trey's voice had lowered to a seductive screen idol tone.

No way. The only thing worse than Ryan putting the

moves on the Tanner troubleshooter would be his crew chief putting the moves on her.

"Trey, if you'll excuse us, we've got business to discuss." Ryan nodded his head toward the chair that Trey had recently vacated.

Trey's eyes narrowed, but his grin didn't fade. "Sure, boss, whatever you say. Did I mention I got you another hour of practice tomorrow morning?"

"Good. I don't want to get stuck in the back of the pack because of a crummy qualifying time." He slugged down his soda before turning to Jamie. "You'll get that motor pulled ASAP?"

"Absolutely."

Hopefully, she would rise to the challenge. Because failure wasn't an option. His whole career was on the line.

CHAPTER THREE

JAMIE WIPED the sweat from her eyes. She'd barely removed the engine and swung the hoist back into place when Trey came to the shop.

"Good, you're done," he commented, stepping too close for Jamie's comfort.

She refused to back away, though. With over a decade in the corporate world, Jamie wasn't a stranger to power plays and questionable advances. She just wasn't sure yet which category Trey Walker fell into.

"Yes, it's freed up for your crew if you want to work on the setup. I ought to be out of the way over there." She nodded toward the far work bench where the engine now rested.

"That'll be fine."

"Ryan said I could use the shop tools. I'll have mine shipped if necessary. I'm hoping it doesn't come to that."

"Hey, that's what we all want." He grinned and winked. "You'll be fine over there. Out of the guys' line of sight."

"What's that supposed to mean?"

He shrugged. "Nothing. Just that you could be… distracting."

Jamie sighed. She'd had him pegged all wrong. Trey was just a run-of-the-mill jerk. "Mr. Walker, your crew will take their cue from you. If you treat me with respect, the other men will, too."

"She's absolutely right." Ryan stood in the doorway, his arms crossed.

"Hey, I'm just pointing out the obvious."

"I expect you to encourage the crew to be professional around Jamie. And I'll hold you responsible if there's trouble."

Trey's grin faded. "Okay, boss. Understood loud and clear. I'll radio the guys to get started on setup."

"Good."

Trey ambled off, seemingly unaffected by Ryan's lecture.

"Ryan, I appreciate you wanting to make things easier for me." Jamie wiped her hands on a towel. "But in the future, please let me fight my own battles. Respect is earned, not dictated. All you've managed to do is make sure everyone knows I need special treatment."

Ryan frowned. "I didn't mean it that way. My team's small, but it's top-notch. I guess I didn't want you to think we were a bunch of yokels."

"I know better. You and your crew didn't get this far by doing things halfway. Besides, there are as many drivers from California as Charlotte. The old yokel stereotype doesn't hold true."

He laughed, his eyes alight. "You're not kidding. Sure, racing's got guys with strong Southern roots, but we've also got young guns from all over the US."

"And where do you fall?"

"In a class all my own." His grin was cocky, but his gaze was serious.

"And what class would that be?"

"I guess I'd call myself an old gun. I don't fit in with the old guard even though I have a traditional approach. And I'm too rough around the edges to hang out with the wine and cigar-bar type."

Jamie was intrigued in spite of herself. She could relate to the feeling of being on the outside looking in. "Sounds like it takes courage."

"Nope. Just plain stubbornness." He nodded toward the tool chest. "You find everything you need?"

Obviously, confidences were over. "Yes, thanks. I better get started tearing down."

"If you need anything, give me a holler. Or Trey. He has a big mouth, but he's a good guy."

"I'll try to remember that."

He nodded and strode away.

Soon, Jamie lost herself in the tear-down process. There was something reassuring in the rote disassembly of an engine. Removing parts, cleaning and setting them aside in a definite pattern for reassembly. It was like a huge, three-dimensional jigsaw puzzle that never ceased to fascinate her no matter how many engines she worked on.

Jamie barely noticed when the crew came in to set up the suspension. The good natured joking and trash talk between men who worked closely together was a familiar background noise that merely made Jamie feel at home. This was where she was meant to be.

"Hey, who's hogging the nine-sixteenths?" an older guy asked. "There should be several of them."

"Well, they must've grown legs, cause there's only one here and I'm using it." The kid didn't look much older than eighteen.

Jamie selected a wrench from her personal set and walked over to the car. "You can use mine." She handed it to the older guy.

He accepted with a grunt. "Thanks. You sure it's not one of ours?"

"Not unless yours has J.T. etched on the handle."

The man flipped over the wrench and squinted. "Guess you're right. You're Jamie Tanner?"

"Yes."

"I knew your daddy when you were just a kid following on his heels."

Jamie grinned. "Taught me everything he knows."

"Well, you should be the best then." The man extended his hand. His callused grip was strong, sure. "Bill Sinclair."

"Good to meet you, Bill. I think my dad's talked about you. You're pretty handy with a wrench yourself."

"How's he doing? Heard he had a heart attack."

Jamie swallowed the lump in her throat. She'd been so intent on her job, she'd forgotten to call home. "He's recovering. They did a quadruple bypass."

"Would you tell him I'm thinkin' of him?"

"You bet."

His voice was gruff. "And thanks for the wrench. I'll make sure it gets right back to you."

"No problem."

Jamie returned to her engine, trying to recall the other things her dad had said about Bill Sinclair. He'd been a top mechanic who'd fallen on hard times after his wife left him. Started drinking and gambling and lost everything. His home, his job and very nearly his health. It looked like he'd turned things around.

It also appeared that Ryan Pearce had given the man a second chance. Maybe she'd been hasty jumping to the conclusion that Pearce was just another hotshot driver.

Jamie frowned as she checked the fuel pump. It looked good. She would have sworn that was the problem. Not a brand she remembered her dad using, but it had been twelve years since she'd worked in his shop.

Setting the pump aside, she wished there was time for a total teardown. The valves would have to wait, especially since the compression was good.

"What'd you find?" Ryan's voice made her jump. "Sorry, didn't mean to sneak up on you again."

"That's just it. I haven't found anything."

"I'd hoped it was something simple and you'd repaired it already."

She raised an eyebrow. "If it was that simple, Bill would have found it and I wouldn't be here."

"True."

"The fuel pump looks good. The compression on the cylinders is good. I don't think the valves are involved. I'd like to see you run in qualifying tomorrow."

"I want it fixed tonight."

It was like trying to talk to a brick wall. "So do I. But we've got a difficult-to-diagnose problem and I need to check all the variables. It might take patience."

"Patience won't make up the points I need to be in

the top ten. I need a good starting position Saturday night and to do that I'll have to kick butt qualifying. I expect you to make sure I have a car that'll perform."

She raised her chin. "I'll do my best. But intermittent failures rarely cooperate with a deadline."

No, they tended to occur at the most critical times. And she feared Ryan Pearce might make her the scapegoat if he didn't do well tomorrow, whether there was a legitimate mechanical failure or not.

JAMIE CALLED room service and ordered a late supper. She wanted to catch the kitchen before it closed.

In Arkansas, her mother would be just arriving home from the hospital.

Removing her cell from her duffel bag, she flipped it open and called the familiar number. Her folks had lived in the same house for almost forty years.

Jamie rubbed the tension from her forehead while the phone rang. She was starting to worry, then her mother picked up.

"Mom, it's me. Is everything okay?"

"Yes, dear. Your father's progressing as well as can be expected. He's still very weak."

"You sound tired."

"I am. I try to stay with Jimmy as long as the staff will allow."

"You need to take care of yourself, too, not just Daddy."

"I'm fine."

"Let me put it another way. You won't be any good to Daddy if you end up sick."

There was silence for a moment.

Her mother's voice was husky when she said, "It means a lot to know you care."

"I've always cared, Mom." Her vision blurred. Life had taken on new meaning since she'd heard her father had almost died. She ached to find the magic formula that would earn her family's approval *and* allow her to stay true to herself.

"I know you have, honey. You just have a hard time showing it sometimes."

Jamie cleared her throat. "How's Daddy doing with his therapy?"

"Stubborn as a mule. But he's finally gotten it through his thick skull they won't release him till he does what they say. He's a model patient now."

"Daddy's strong-willed all right."

"How are *you* doing, honey?"

"Okay. I haven't located the problem yet, but I'm hoping to know more after qualifying tomorrow."

"I'm sure you will. You were always very knowledgeable."

Her grudging admission gave Jamie hope.

"Mom?"

"Yes?"

"I…want to do things differently while I'm at home this time. I want to make it work."

"I do, too, dear."

Jamie was heartened by her mother's attitude, until later in bed that night, when she realized her mother's admission could have meant a number of things.

RYAN PULLED his uniform on over his long johns and fastened it. He'd bet only the forty-two other drivers would be wearing layers of synthetic fabrics, with this heat. But safety came first, comfort second. Fortunately, qualifying would be short and he wouldn't have to sweat his rear off like he undoubtedly would in the main race.

He left his motor home, nodded to another driver and headed toward the hauler.

Trey and Bill were engrossed in the computer atop the pit cart. They barely glanced up from the monitor as Ryan approached.

"We good to go?" Ryan asked.

"Yep." Trey closed the file. "We made those adjustments you wanted. Shouldn't get loose anymore."

"Good. Tanner here yet?"

"Yeah, she's in the shop. Reassembling the motor. Seems to know what she's doing."

Bill frowned. "Of course she knows what she's doing. The girl's got motor oil in her veins. Her dad's the best there is and she takes after him."

Ryan stretched, relieved to hear Bill's assessment. "You get a chance to watch her yesterday?"

"Sure did. That gal's gifted. Don't know why Jimmy Tanner didn't have her run the shop from the get-go."

"Tom Tanner's competent. And word has it Jimmy won't ever retire."

"Nope. That old goat'll have to be taken out in a body bag." There was a trace of admiration in Bill's voice. "Although that heart attack came darn close."

Ryan knew Bill had been to hell and back and didn't impress easily. That meant Jimmy Tanner had earned every bit of his reputation.

"I'm going to grab a drink and head over to the garage."

"Hey, Ryan?" Trey grinned.

"What?"

"You're going to regret those long johns and uniform. Jamie Tanner is hot, hot, hot."

Ryan rolled his eyes. He was just about to remind Trey to behave when Bill spoke.

"You treat the lady with respect. I might just need to step in for her daddy and whup your butt."

"Yeah, you and what army, old man?" Trey's words were tough, but he stepped back a pace.

"Trey and I have already talked about this. He'll be on his best behavior," Ryan said.

Trey grunted.

Ryan went inside the hauler and grabbed a sports drink from the refrigerator. He ignored Trey and Bill's squabbling as he walked past them and headed to the shop, wishing he could jog a couple of laps. The nervous energy was building.

Because so much rode on getting a good position for the main race, qualifying usually made him feel like he might puke. And, as Craig Blake, the team owner, had pointed out in their most recent meeting, this race was make it or break it. The sponsors were ticked off about having their logo splashed across the hood of a losing car.

Ryan shaded his eyes as he approached the shop, easily spotting the Tanner logo, where Jamie stood next to the work table. But it wasn't the green T-shirt that held his attention. It was Jamie's look of concentration. She almost vibrated with the intensity of her focus—something he'd noticed with most of the truly gifted mechanics. The process was organic, but a smart mechanic never took it for granted. It was an exchange of energy, a meshing of sorts.

"How's it going?" Ryan asked as he entered the garage. The shade was a welcome relief after his short walk.

She glanced up. "I wish I had something definitive to tell you."

"What's your gut instinct?"

"Everything looks good. Ignition and electrical are two areas that can mimic others. Did you transfer to your backup ignition box after you noticed the problems?"

"No. Come to think of it, that might explain why it's so hard to pin down. If it's intermittent, sometimes the spark is amplified, sometimes not."

"That's what I think. Is your backup box new?"

"Nope. You may have noticed this is a bare bones operation. We get the most possible miles out of our equipment while trying to stay competitive."

"Let's change out the ignition box for qualifying and see if that takes care of it."

"Will do. I'll help you."

When she started to protest, he raised his hand. "I'll just assist. With two of us it'll go faster."

"I don't like owners or drivers involved in my work. It gets sticky."

"Hey, I turned wrenches for a living before I started driving full-time."

"Sure you did." She tilted her head to the side, grinning. "Even the guys at Lightning Lube turn wrenches."

Ryan didn't know whether to be insulted or amused.

He decided to be amused. “I assure you, I was no maintenance mechanic. I worked at a corner repair shop. If it broke, we fixed it.”

“Okay, Slick. I’ll give you one chance. But you do anything stupid, no more helping or suggesting. The garage will be off limits.”

He laughed. “As if you could throw me out of my own garage.”

“Actually, the garage is owned by the track. And the car is owned by Craig Blake. So, buddy, out there,” she pointed to the track, where the stands were already filling, “you might be hot stuff. But in here, *I’m* the boss.”

Ryan’s gut tightened in protest. Either he’d just met his match or his pre-qualifying jitters had ratcheted up a notch. He sure hoped it was the jitters. Otherwise, he was in serious trouble. Because he liked a woman who didn’t take BS from anyone.

CHAPTER FOUR

JAMIE SAT atop the pit box, her prime seat courtesy of Bill. Watching through binoculars, she had a perfect view of the track.

She held her breath as the Number 63 car took off. There didn't seem to be anything wrong today. It looked like Ryan quickly found his line and worked it for all it was worth. No hesitation in the turns like yesterday. That meant one of two things. Either the problem had been fixed when they'd changed out the ignition box or Ryan was an inconsistent driver.

Jamie released a breath as she watched him effortlessly coax everything the machine had to give. Below her, Trey counted off the time, his voice getting more excited as they went.

It was a good run. A damn good run.

Her mood soared. The problem was solved. She could go home a hero, having saved the day for Team 63.

But on the heels of victory, doubt crept in. What if there had been something in addition to the box? Intermittent problems were tricky.

Trey and Bill hooted and hollered when their car came in.

The guys ran out to meet Ryan at the pit, Jamie following close behind. He unhooked the window netting and maneuvered himself out the window. Removing his helmet, he grinned. "Now that's the way a car should handle."

Trey slapped him on the back. "You nailed it."

"Nice run," Bill said.

Ryan glanced up and caught Jamie's gaze.

She stepped forward. "You looked good out there. No problem with loss of power?"

"Nope. I had my foot on it and the car responded."

"Great. Looks like you've got a shot at pole position."

"All I ask is a chance. With the car set up right and the problem solved, I can run up front."

Jamie nodded. But she was just superstitious enough to wish he hadn't declared the problem solved. "All the same, I'll stay on until after the race Saturday night."

"Sure. It's your dime—not mine."

Wincing inside, she hoped she wouldn't get a fiscal dressing-down from Tom. "I'd like to see you practice before the race, too."

"Thanks. I appreciate your dedication."

Jamie shrugged. "Hey, it means I can take in the NASCAR Busch Series race."

"Come on by the hauler before the race—you can watch with us from the roof if you want." His smile was wide. With the pressure off for twenty-four hours, he could apparently afford to be generous.

She felt herself respond to his easy charm all the same. "Thanks. I'd like that."

"See you later then."

"Okay."

Jamie headed for the garage, where she grabbed her tool duffel and slung the strap over her shoulder. The drive to her hotel was uneventful. With half a day to herself, what was she to do?

Her cell rang as she opened the door to her hotel room.

Glancing at the display, she flipped it open. "Hey, Tom. You catch Pearce qualifying?"

"Yeah. Looked good."

"I think I've got it taken care of. We changed out the ignition box."

"That would explain the loss of power. You coming home tonight?"

"No, after the race."

"You trying to schedule R & R already?" Though his tone was joking, there was an underlying edge.

"I'm being thorough. Isn't that what you wanted?"

"Of course. Just don't go wild with the expense account."

Jamie squelched a rush of irritation. "First it was 'Jamie, pull our cookies out of the fire.' Now that I've done that, all of a sudden you're concerned about the bottom line."

"I'm always concerned about the bottom line. You've got the hotel room for another night. After that, it comes out of your pocket. And why don't you hang out at the Pearce hauler? You can eat his food instead of using your expense account."

"You know what, Tom? You've turned into a total bean counter." It was the worst insult she could imagine.

Apparently Tom didn't think so, because there was

a smile in his voice when he said, "I prefer to think of it as careful."

Jamie couldn't help but grin in response. "I have to give you your due. All that penny-pinching has paid off. Dad says you've managed to grow the company pretty well."

"What can I say? It's a gift. Doesn't mean I want to take over all the admin, though."

"Perish the thought. Can't say that I blame you. I'd better go."

"One thing first, Sis."

"What?"

"Good job."

"Thanks." Jamie slowly shut her phone, trying not to let his praise get to her. But pride warmed her all the same. They might just make a team after all.

RYAN CLOSED his eyes and savored the relative peace as he kicked back in a folding chair on the reinforced roof of the hauler.

"Is he dead?" a female voice asked.

He cranked open one eye to view Jamie standing over him. Bill stood off to the side, grinning.

"Some law against a guy relaxing?"

"No. But I got the impression you were Type A through and through."

He nodded toward a chair. "Have a seat. Would you believe me if I said I was meditating?"

She snorted and sat down. "I don't think so. You don't impress me as the creative visualization type."

"You've got me pegged. But I've learned I can't have that adrenaline rush going 24/7."

She tilted her head. "Very wise. Some drivers never learn. When'd you start racing?"

"Not till my twenties. I didn't get really serious until I was almost thirty."

Jamie raised an eyebrow. "Nearly ancient."

"By today's standards, yeah. I see these young guys—so much more focused than I was at their age. But then again, I worked full-time at construction or as a mechanic. That doesn't leave a whole lotta energy left over at the end of the day."

"Agreed." She turned her head, glancing around the deck. Her blond ponytail swished with the movement.

"Where's your Pistons hat?"

"Huh?" Adjusting the stiff brim of her Tanner cap, she said, "I'm humoring my brother by becoming a walking billboard. Family pride and all that. And the possibility of a little free advertising to offset the extra hotel charge."

"Tight budget?"

"No. Just the usual controlling, penny-pinching stuff."

"That's why I couldn't work with family." He mentally winced at the thought of his mom being in charge of any aspect of his life.

"Brothers and sisters?"

"No, just me and Mom."

"Say no more. If I allowed my mom control in my life, I'd be a beauty contestant trying to hook a *suitable* man."

"What's she consider suitable?"

"Someone with the potential of being a pillar of the community. Polished, successful, a real draw at the country club. Oh, and a good Southern Baptist. I'm a huge disappointment to her." She shrugged, a trace of wistfulness in her eyes.

He thought her mother must be awfully shortsighted not to be proud of her daughter just the way she was. Unique, talented and smart. "Let me guess. Pillars of the community are squeamish about women with grease under their fingernails?"

"That and they generally don't understand my total obsession with racing." She leaned back in her chair. "How about your mom? What would she want you to do?"

"Anything but racing." The answer was out before he could stop it.

"I bet that makes for some uncomfortable family dinners."

"Not really. It's always there, unspoken. Like the elephant in the living room."

"I guess we all have our elephants, huh?"

Ryan shifted in his chair. Lord knew he had a whole herd of them. "There's soda over there in the cooler. We don't stock alcohol. I don't like to encourage drinking at the track even if we're technically off duty right now. I want my crew to know, first and foremost, this is our job."

Her eyes sparkled with mischief. "That sounds very Type A."

"Just good business. The liability issues get complex."

"I think I'll take you up on that soda. You want anything?"

"Nope. I'm good. I've got a meeting with Craig Blake, the owner, in a couple minutes. Need to enjoy the peace while it lasts."

"He ought to be happy about your qualifying time."

"Yeah, but he wants more. I hope to deliver at the race."

"We all want that," she threw over her shoulder as she walked away.

Ryan leaned back and closed his eyes slightly. He watched Jamie from beneath his half-closed eyelids. She moved with an athletic grace, managing to appear feminine without a bunch of cosmetics and skimpy clothes.

She stopped and chatted with Bill and Trey, laughing at something Bill said. Her wide smile made him pause. He hadn't thought of her too much as a woman before now. Just another tech who may or may not help save his racing career.

Straightening, he opened his eyes and gave up the pretense of being relaxed.

Focus, Ryan, focus.

The coming meeting would be tricky at best and the last thing he needed was to be distracted trying to figure out Jamie Tanner. Or wondering what she looked like beneath the tight T-shirt.

When she returned, he glanced at his watch. "I better go prepare for my meeting. Enjoy the race."

"Thanks. Enjoy your meeting."

"Yep. Like a root canal." He climbed down the ladder and went to the lounge in the hauler. It was blessedly empty. Craig hadn't yet arrived.

Grabbing the latest stats off the table, he eyed the figures. They were damn good. It was early in the season—if he finished well in the next couple of races, he could make up lost ground.

Ryan just hoped like hell Jamie Tanner was right and his car was in top-notch shape.

JAMIE RESTED her forearms on the railing encircling the roof of the hauler. The roar of performance engines pushed to the max made her pulse pound.

They were halfway through the NASCAR Busch Series race and still no sign of Ryan. Frowning, she tried to put it out of her mind. She'd done her part to make sure he would win. The rest was up to him.

Jamie was distracted by the sight of the front-runner coming up on the lapped back of the pack. Getting around the slower cars could be tricky.

Two cars collided. She inhaled sharply. One went high. The other spun and then coasted harmlessly into the infield.

The crowd cheered when both drivers exited their vehicles and appeared to be fine. She knew they would be checked out by the on-site doctors anyway.

Bill stepped beside her. "It's a good day when everyone walks away. Wasn't always that way in the old days."

"They've come a long way safety-wise in the twenty years since I hung out in the pits with Dad."

"Yep. You going back to Tanner later today?"

"Sunday morning. I want to catch Ryan's race tomorrow night."

"Maybe he'll show you what he's made of. His last couple of runs haven't done him justice."

"That's what he says."

"He's not just blowing smoke. Ryan doesn't brag. He tells it like it is. He'll be the first one to admit when he screws up, too."

Jamie wondered why it seemed so important for Bill to convince her. "If you say he's good, I believe you."

"I've been around NASCAR since the late seventies. I can tell a driver with talent. And I can tell a mechanic with talent. You've done a good job here. Your daddy couldn't have done better."

His praise left a lump in her throat. What she wouldn't give for her father to say something like that. Or, better yet, her mom. She squeezed Bill's scarred, callused hand resting on the rail. "Thanks."

"Just give him a chance." He nodded toward Ryan, who returned to the roof. Pushing away from the rail, Bill walked away.

Jamie frowned, watching him go. Strange conversation.

"Why the frown?"

"Just wondering what's going on with Bill. He was pretty insistent on telling me what a great driver you are. And a straight shooter."

"Hey, I should see about getting him a bonus out of the PR budget."

Nodding, Jamie tried to brush off the conversation.

"He's loyal, Jamie. Maybe he has some strange idea that he needs to pay me back by talking me up to nonbelievers."

"He owes you?"

"Only in his mind. Sure, I gave him a chance when others didn't. I pushed for him to be hired. But he's a damn good mechanic. And when he told me he'd dealt with his demons, I believed him. Now, update me on the race. I've got a few friends out there."

She quickly brought him up-to-speed.

There was longing in his eyes as he watched the track.

"Is it strange for you to see the race from up here, when you're so used to being down there?"

"A little. But mostly it's nostalgia. I remember I was scared to death my first Busch race. Puked my guts up. But now, it seems like a pretty good time. Not as much pressure."

"You'll settle in."

"I *have* to settle in. This is all I've ever wanted. And there's no way I'm gonna blow it." The intensity in his voice didn't surprise her. The desperation did.

CHAPTER FIVE

LAUGHTER AND JOKES swirled around Jamie as the men discussed their plans for the evening. Ryan's buddy had won the race, so he'd gone to congratulate him.

Jamie hesitated, wondering if she should go to her hotel room and order room service. The idea was monumentally unappealing.

"Hey, Jamie, we're gonna go grab something to eat at a sports bar not far from here. Wanna come?" Bill asked.

Bless the crusty, kind-hearted man. "Sure. Can I follow you?"

"You bet. Ryan should be back any minute. You mind giving him a ride? There's no room in my rental truck and the drivers are pretty leery of getting on Sheriff Joe's bad side."

Jamie laughed. "Sure." She was still smiling when Ryan returned.

Bill was quick to advise him of the transportation arrangements. Ryan raised an eyebrow, but didn't comment.

"My car's this way. You won't critique my driving, will you?" She jangled her keys.

"Not if I can help it. But don't take it personally if I'm quiet. Being a passenger makes me nervous."

"It's a rental or I'd let you drive."

"That's okay. I'll be on my best behavior. You drive and I'll pretend being a passenger doesn't bother me."

"Wow, what a ringing endorsement of my skills."

"Call me a control freak, but that's just the way I am."

"I imagine it's the same for pilots when they fly as passengers. Occupational hazard."

They reached Jamie's car. She unlocked the doors and slid in on the driver's side.

Ryan got in, pushing the passenger seat back to accommodate his long legs.

She followed Bill's truck, trying not to be self-conscious about her driving. They chatted about the NASCAR Busch series race and debated strategies of the various teams.

"Regular roadways must seem like a snail's pace to you."

"Yeah. But I'm glad you're not like some people who think they have to impress me with their street-racing skills."

"As if I could do that. I'm not that competitive. Now, start messing around my shop, that's a different story."

"Why does that not surprise me?" He adjusted the headrest. "Is your dad like Bill?"

"Bill reminds me a bit of my dad. Same intolerance for BS and people who don't do their jobs right. But an old softy inside."

"Yep. You've got Bill nailed."

She wondered if going to a bar would be a problem for the older man, but didn't know how to broach the subject. If Ryan hadn't already heard the stories circulating about Bill's past, she certainly didn't want to tell him. But she couldn't help worrying just the same.

"What's the problem?"

"Problem?"

"You were frowning again."

"I was thinking I meant to call Dad today." It was the truth. Just not the whole truth.

They pulled into the parking lot of a small sports bar, where there were only a few spaces available. Bill and the rest of the guys waited near the door.

Jamie fleetingly wondered if the wily old guy had been matchmaking. Shaking her head, she told herself this was a simple meal among colleagues, nothing more. She was pleased to be included all the same, because it meant they accepted her.

The bar was packed. Roughhewn wood beams, sports memorabilia from various teams on the wall—it could have been a sports bar anywhere. The clientele on the other hand was an interesting combination of rednecks and yuppies. With no visible rancor, the two groups seemed to coexist. And, thankfully, only a few turned to watch as they walked in.

The guys found two recently vacated tables near the back and pushed them together. Jamie selected a seat near Bill. Ryan took the seat opposite her.

"Trey didn't want to come with us?" she asked.

Ryan shrugged. "Nah. Said he had some paperwork to do."

The waitress brought menus. The usual fare—burgers, sandwiches, steaks. Jamie was pleasantly surprised to see a nice selection of salads.

She ordered a sirloin, salad and grilled veggies.

Ryan ordered the same, but added a baked potato and French fries.

Jamie tilted her head. "Carb loading?"

"Something like that. I'll eat light tomorrow."

"Are evening races hard for you? The change in routine and all?"

"Better than racing when it's a hundred degrees. That'd put the interior temperature at something like a hundred and forty."

"Yeah, I'd take night racing, too, if I were you."

"Hey, Jamie, rumor has it you designed minivans." One of the guys—Brice or Brent—said. She had a heck of a time remembering which was which. Each looked as if he might have just graduated from high school. "What's a nice girl like you doing in a place like this?"

"The same reason you're not a mechanic in some dealership. I was born to build performance engines. I did the other stuff because I thought I was supposed to."

Brent or Brice nodded. "Yeah. I can relate. I was supposed to be an accountant."

Ryan leaned forward. "Did you quit your job, Jamie? Are you with Tanner for the long haul?"

Jamie hesitated. She didn't want him to think she wasn't dedicated because of a short-term gig. "I have a contract with Tanner. I'm technically on vacation from my other employer until my buyout packet is processed."

"I read something about them offering incentives. Seems like a no-brainer to be back at Tanner."

Yes, a no-brainer. Unless, of course, you'd been betrayed by your family. "I'm sure it'll turn out fine," she said to reassure herself as much to reassure him.

He nodded and brought up the next evening's race.

Soon the debate was hot and heavy over which teams had set up their cars for peak performance. Which driver was the hothead. Which driver was the new one to watch.

For the first time in years, Jamie felt totally accepted.

As if reading her mind, Ryan commented, "I bet this is a lot different than hanging out with a bunch of engineers."

She grinned. "*Much* different. In a good way. I made some of the other engineers uncomfortable, probably because I wanted to go beyond the theoretical. I wanted to make sure what we designed transferred into the real world. And that it actually worked when everything was said and done, not just on paper."

"You're a gearhead, honey, one of us." Bill patted her hand.

Had anyone at her prior job called her honey, she would have made them sorry. Very sorry. But coming from Bill, prefaced with *gearhead,* it was definitely a promotion.

"And then there was my need for speed. A four-banger with an automatic tranny was so not my idea of an optimum vehicle."

Ryan threw back his head and laughed. "I bet the suits just loved that."

For once, it did seem humorous. Realizing how totally incompatible she'd been with the corporate world. "No, they didn't. But I won them enough awards for innovative design to keep my job. And I was able to design a bulletproof engine with more bang for the buck. But it still wasn't enough to save the division." The thought rankled.

"Hey, don't take it personally. You were only one person in the middle of big business."

"You're absolutely right. That's why being at Tanner Motors again is so refreshing. In my dad's shop, I'll have ultimate responsibility for every product that goes out the door. And I'll work my butt off to make sure it's a success."

Ryan held up his hand. "I believe you, I believe you."

"You've got your daddy's fire, Jamie. And your mama's stick-to-it-iveness. I see big things in your future," Bill said.

Warmth spread through her. She felt like a sponge, soaking up the understanding and comraderie.

"Steak, medium rare." The waitress put a large platter in front of Jamie, then quickly served the rest of the table.

The conversation grew sporadic as everyone dug in—everyone, but Bill that is. He closed his eyes for a moment and murmured a blessing.

When he opened his eyes, he caught her watching him. He winked and grinned.

She smiled, relieved to see that she'd been worried for nothing. Nobody at the table drank anything harder than cola. And even if they'd been chugging beer, somehow Jamie thought Bill would have been okay. He seemed…centered.

Tilting her head, she asked Ryan, "No drinking off-track, either?"

"Not until after the race. The guys know that when they sign on with my crew. It saves headaches and heart-aches. And ensures we're one hundred percent focused on race day."

Jamie ate in silence, processing what she'd learned about Ryan Pearce. He didn't make excuses, but he believed in second chances. He wasn't just a driver, he was the team's leader. And he was more grounded than she'd ever imagined.

She enjoyed his company, enjoyed the company of his crew. When she went home Sunday, she'd feel as if she was leaving friends behind. What more could she ask?

"You're Ryan Pearce, aren't you?" A thirtyish guy in khakis and a golf shirt slapped Ryan on the shoulder.

Ryan's hand clenched, but his smile didn't falter. "Yes, I am."

"Hey, would you sign this napkin for me? Say, 'For my buddy, Skip.'" The man thrust a napkin and pen at Ryan.

"Sure." He shrugged almost imperceptibly, scrawling his name after the requested phrase. "Here you go, Skip."

The man slapped him on the shoulder again. Ryan stiffened.

Jamie held her breath. She'd seen men in bars get decked for less obvious invasions of personal space.

"Thanks, man. I'll be rooting for you tomorrow night."

"You're welcome. I appreciate the good thoughts."

Jamie glanced around the table. Everyone continued eating.

"Do you have many uninterrupted meals?"

"Sometimes." He touched her hand, his eyes warm with concern. "I'm sorry, I don't even give it a second thought anymore. Did it bother you?"

His concern surprised her. And made her want to know Ryan Pearce the person, not just the driver. "It doesn't bother me as long as I'm not the one they want to talk to. It must feel kind of strange, though, all those people who feel like they know you."

"The fans are great. They're the ones who buy tickets to the races and support me every step of the way. A few interrupted meals are a small price to pay. But it's not always fair to the people I'm with, dividing my attention that way."

Jamie got the impression it was a woman he referred to. It made her wonder if he'd tried to mix a relationship with racing and failed.

"It's a part of your job. I understand."

His expression was thoughtful. "Yes, you've been around racing enough, you probably do."

Then the discussion turned to racing, inspiring a heated debate on the merits of restrictor plates. Jamie found the discussion invigorating.

After staunchly defending the practice as leveling the playing field, she turned to find Ryan watching her. Her face grew warm. There was something different about his gaze, an intensity that made her nerves sizzle.

"What?" she demanded.

"You're smiling again."

"What's so odd about that? I smile a lot."

"I've just never met a woman who felt that passionately about restrictor plates. It's…interesting."

Jamie rolled her eyes. "That's another way of saying weird."

"Not for this bunch it isn't." He leaned forward, holding her gaze. "I meant it as a compliment."

"Oh. Um, thanks." Wasn't that an awkward response. For once, she wished for an ounce of her mother's social grace. "I mean, well, other people aren't so enlightened."

"Darlin', you've been hanging out with the wrong crowd." His wicked grin surprised her.

And the way she felt compelled to watch his lips as *darlin'* rolled off his tongue was downright scary.

Shaking her head, Jamie realized she could be in deep trouble.

RYAN RELEASED a breath as they entered the track parking lot. His stint as a passenger was almost over, along with his trip of discovery. He'd found that in addition to being a 'hottie', as Trey had described her, Jamie Tanner was one smart woman. She could talk racing all night long and had a smile that could make any man a fan of restrictor plates.

"Would you mind pulling around back?" he asked.

"Security will let me?"

"As long as you're with me."

Jamie grinned. "Ooh, I love a man with connections."

She stopped the car at the entrance to the motor home lot.

A guard stepped out from the shadows.

Ryan was tempted to invite her to his place. Nothing sexual. Just to talk.

Yeah, right.

"I can walk from here. Thanks for the ride."

"Sure. See you tomorrow."

He got out. "You can watch from the hauler if you want. Maybe wear some headphones so you can hear us?"

She nodded. "Thanks, I'd like that. I know you'll be busy, so I'll wish you luck tonight."

"Thanks." He nodded and tapped the hood of her car before walking through the gates.

Ryan resisted the temptation to turn and watch her drive away. He needed to get his head on straight and concentrate on the race tomorrow.

CHAPTER SIX

JAMIE ENTERED the hauler early the next evening. It was deserted, except for a stunning redhead. She ignored a twinge of emotion she didn't want to identify. If Ryan had a girlfriend, wouldn't she have heard about her? Maybe, maybe not.

The woman extended her hand. "I'm Sheila, Trey's girlfriend. I flew in for the race."

Trey's girlfriend. The news made Jamie surprisingly happy.

"How'd practice go this morning?"

"Good. Trey thinks they've got the car dialed in."

"I'm glad to hear it. Ryan said I could watch from upstairs." She pointed heavenward. "And wear a team headset."

"I wear foam ear plugs. The headsets mess up my hair. I wanted to sit on the pit box, but Trey said I'd be too much of a distraction." The redhead smiled, primping her hair. "I'm going upstairs if you want to come."

"Sure." Jamie selected a headset out of the cabinet and followed Sheila outside.

As she climbed the steep aluminum steps attached to the side of the hauler, she wonder how Sheila managed in three-inch stacked heels.

But manage she did and Jamie felt like the ugly stepsister next to Sheila's lush beauty.

Jamie selected a folding chair and sat on the edge of it. She was too nervous to sit back, but didn't want to freak out the other woman by pacing the length of the hauler.

They chatted politely for a few minutes, then lapsed into silence, pretending to be enthralled by the pre-race happenings on the track below.

Glancing at the woman's exquisite jewelry and designer jeans, Jamie doubted they had anything in common. But her mom had raised her to be polite. "That's a beautiful ring."

Sheila held out her hand and admired the rock—er, diamond. "My ex-fiancé insisted I keep it after we broke up."

"Hmm. Nice guy." Jamie wondered what Trey thought about that.

Jamie felt she'd done her social duty, so she didn't rush to fill the void when silence fell again. Instead, she studied the track.

Ryan had received second position. On the outside, he started shoulder to shoulder with the pole winner. It was a good way to begin what could be a long evening.

When the drivers were introduced, Jamie couldn't sit still a moment longer. She went to the rail, her heart in her throat when the honored guest, a local business leader, announced, *"Drivers start your engines."*

It seemed to take forever as they slowly followed behind the pace car. Then the green flag was lowered—the roar was almost deafening.

Ryan and the pole car battled for first place. Ryan won. Sheila cheered.

Jamie merely chewed on her fingernails, aware that an early lead meant nothing in a race of five hundred miles.

Another car came up on the outside, claiming the lead.

Nodding, Jamie smiled as Ryan settled in on the guy's bumper, drafting. The former pole car pulled in behind Ryan. This tight formation of the first three cars would serve them well in the coming laps if they could maintain it. The sharing of airflow would allow them all to gain speed and save fuel. It promised to be a fast race from the looks of it.

Jamie dialed in the Pearce team frequency on her headset and listened to the chatter between Trey and Ryan. Ryan sounded relaxed and happy with the way the car handled. Then a car following the lead group got loose in Turn Two and collided with another car.

The yellow flag came out. Ryan's spotter piped up on the headset to guide him around the cars and debris. The resulting pit stop went smooth as silk and Ryan's Number 63 car retained his position.

The race settled in and so did Jamie. She figured Ryan had a good chance of winning—he handled the car with power, grace and heart. Despite her doubts, he was proving he had what it took to be a champion. She was grateful the problem with the ignition box had been found in time.

Sheila touched her shoulder, holding out a bottle of water. "Want one?"

Jamie pulled her headset down to hang around her neck. "Thanks." She realized she was sticky with perspiration. Nerves? More like the night time temperature that was still in the eighties.

"How long have you and Ryan been, you know, involved?" Sheila asked.

"Me? And Ryan? No, it's not like that. I'm trouble shooting for Tanner Motors. We built his engine."

"Yes, I know." The redhead glanced at her sideways. "But you seem awfully nervous. I thought maybe it was more than the engine."

"It's an important race."

"Oh."

Jamie wracked her brain for common ground, but couldn't find any. "So, um, have you and Trey been together long?"

"Three months. I wanted to fly in last night but he told me not to. Had to make adjustments on some ignition box or something."

"But—" Jamie clamped her mouth shut. They had already replaced the ignition box. Trey was probably dodging too much quality time with his sweetie.

Sheila chattered on about Trey and how she was "so into him." Jamie tuned her out, then finally put her headset back on. The woman didn't take the hint—it didn't seem to bother her that Jamie wasn't listening.

What seemed like a half-hour later, the front three cars broke formation. It was every man for himself now. Jamie was startled to realize more than three hours had elapsed and there were only twenty laps left in the race.

She held her breath as Ryan made his move to pass the second car. He went high and seemed to have it under control. But then he faltered and dropped back into line several car lengths behind, losing ground in his bid to pass.

Trey's voice crackled on the headset. "Talk to me, Ry. What's going on?"

"I don't know. Car's hesitating again. It feels different this time."

"Switch to the backup box."

"Will do."

Jamie frowned, waiting for Ryan to switch to the backup ignition amplifier box. Both boxes were new.

Cars from behind started to press the Number 63 car and he wasn't able to hold them off.

"It's not working, Trey."

"You need to pit?"

"Let's hope there's a caution. I'm not gonna lose any more ground."

"It's your call, buddy."

"I'll get this sucker moving." But he didn't. He lost more ground.

Then, he was lapped.

Jamie groaned aloud. Ryan was struggling, just trying to maintain a decent finish.

He ended up twenty-sixth.

Definitely not what he'd needed.

RYAN PACED inside the hauler, trying to get his frustration under control. The damn car was cursed. Bad luck. Or was *his* luck just bad?

Shaking his head, he refused to allow paranoia to take over. The car was a total dog. Maybe it was time to cut his losses and demand a new car?

Ryan could just imagine that conversation with the owner. Craig would simply give the ride to someone else. No, Ryan was stuck with this particular problem. He might not be able to get a new car, but he could roll up his sleeves and find out what was wrong with this one.

Decision replaced helplessness. It felt good to be in control again.

Ryan stalked off to the garage where his crew was gathered around the offending vehicle like mourners at a funeral. All they lacked was a casket to be lowered into the ground.

"You all gonna stand there while our team goes down the tubes?"

"Motor's still too hot—you know that." Bill's voice was even.

Ryan sighed. "Yeah, I know. I just need to *do* something. And putting my fist through a wall would be too painful. So I figured I'd come down here and help figure things out."

Trey approached and draped his arm over Ryan's shoulder. "Hey, Ry, buddy, why don't we go get a bottle of tequila and drown our sorrows?"

"That's not the answer."

"Maybe not. But it'll keep you out of these guys' way while they do what they do best." He nodded toward Jamie. "Guys and gal, I mean."

Trey's easygoing manner usually was a good counterbalance to Ryan's intensity. But now it grated.

"Trey, I'm not some kid you can BS. It's my butt on the line. Someone's not getting their job done. Nothing's gone right for the past three races."

Bill wiped his hands on a shop towel. "It happens. You know that as well as I do."

"All I know is, things went downhill once we got that new engine."

Jamie raised her chin. "The ignition box had nothing

to do with our motor. Your crew installed it after the fact. We would have insisted on a new box."

It galled him to admit, if only to himself, she was right. He didn't feel like being fair at the moment. *He* wanted to be right. And he absolutely needed to know his career wasn't over. "It was the motor today. I guarantee it."

"We won't know for sure until we get into it. So why don't you hold off making sweeping statements?"

Her moderation only made him angrier. How could everyone be so calm and reasonable when his life was crumbling?

"I'll be in the motor home. Call me when the engine cools down."

Trey muttered something about hoping Ryan cooled down, too.

Ryan let the comment slide. Otherwise, he'd be tempted to deck his best friend.

The sights and sounds of the track failed to calm him. A few straggling fans asked for autographs and he signed them as he walked.

He breathed a sigh of relief when he reached the motor home lot. Though it was after midnight, couples sat in lawn chairs watching their children play. Some barbecued a late-night supper. Others talked quietly.

It soothed him but made him sad at the same time. He'd never experienced this kind of close-knit family life, thanks to his dad. It had always been just him and his mom. Mom working two jobs to make ends meet, getting more bitter every year. And Ryan pretty much raising himself.

He'd grown, made his own life, tried to be a better

man than his father. But he had no wife and no family to show for his efforts. Instead, he'd dedicated himself to racing. And now, he was in danger of losing the career he'd dreamed of for twenty-eight years.

He couldn't, *wouldn't* let that happen.

CHAPTER SEVEN

RYAN AWOKE to a knock at the motor home door. From his recliner, he blearily eyed the clock. It was two a.m.

The knock sounded again.

"I'm coming." He brought the seat to a vertical position and walked to the door.

He opened it and saw Jamie through the screen.

"The motor cooled off enough now? You didn't have to come all the way over here. You could've called my cell."

"May I come in?"

"Sure." He moved aside to let her in. He was uncomfortable having her there. Then he realized she was the only female he'd been alone with in his motor home other than his mother. Too much temptation otherwise.

Jamie glanced around. "We went ahead and did some initial poking around."

"I told you to call me."

She shrugged. "The guys and I agreed we'd go ahead without you. Nothing personal, Ryan. But sometimes having a driver standing over your shoulder making suggestions can get a little touchy."

"I'm not just any driver. I've got plenty of experience—"

"Turning wrenches. I know, you've told me several times. But a brilliant doctor doesn't diagnose his own illness, a smart lawyer doesn't represent himself."

He folded his arms over his chest. "This isn't brain surgery."

"Sometimes it can be just as delicate. You know that as well as I do. Let me ask you this. How do you feel when people tell you how to drive?"

"It pisses me off."

"It's the same for your crew. No matter how well-meaning you are, sometimes it's better if you don't get elbow-deep under the hood."

Hmm. He'd never thought of it that way before. "I'm just trying to help. An extra set of hands."

"Sometimes it's better to stay hands-off. Now is one of those times."

"So I'm supposed to just stay on the sidelines?" The idea rankled. He was a doer, not a watcher.

"In this situation, yes. The guys need to be able to concentrate and they can't do that with you breathing down their necks."

"They appointed you as spokesperson?"

"Not exactly." She grinned. "I drew the short straw."

"It's Trey's job to coach me and make sure the mechanical end runs smoothly. He should be here."

"And he probably would have been, but we couldn't locate him."

What? Trey's absence bothered him, but he had more important things to worry about. "Out with it. What did you find?"

"Fuel pump. You don't normally see one that new fail, but it happens."

Ryan swore under his breath. "Didn't you inspect it when you did the tear down?"

"Of course I inspected it. The pump appeared in good condition. The housing was intact."

"Apparently you were wrong." Ryan's gut knotted. The whole course of his life hinged on the wear and tear of moving parts. Frustration made him want to lash out. "But you would have known that if you'd been more thorough."

Her eyes flashed, but her voice was coolly professional. "I *was* thorough. The intermittent problems weren't related to the fuel pump. The housing of a brand new part appeared to be fine, so there was no reason to tear it down. Most mechanics would have acted as I did."

"I don't want most mechanics. I want the best." Even as Ryan said it, he knew he was being unfair. But he couldn't seem to take it back.

Jamie's chin came up to its fighting angle. "I *am* the best." She turned and strode to the door. Her hand on the knob, she looked back and said, "I apologize for the part failure—you can bet I'll be talking to the parts rep about it. I'll take the pump back to Tanner with me and go over it in detail. Otherwise, it looks like my work here is done."

"Yes, it does." Phoenix was over, history. He'd have to get his head on straight and strategize for Talladega.

Ryan resisted the urge to slam the door behind Jamie. Resisted the urge to accept his fate and give up.

JAMIE HESITATED at her father's hospital door. Pasting on a carefree smile, she entered.

"Jamie, you're here," her mom said.

"I wrapped it up with the Pearce team, so I thought I'd spend a few hours with my favorite guy. Hi, Daddy, how're you doing?"

He smiled wanly. "I'm still here, aren't I?"

"Is that a complaint about the hospital or relief that you have a second lease on life?"

"Both. I'm ready to go home. A guy can't sleep around here. There's always somebody waking me up to take blood or give me a sleeping pill. Now, if I'm asleep, what do I need a sleeping pill for?"

"You do what they say so you can go home." She stepped over to the bed and grasped his hand. "Then you'll have the best nurse on the planet: Mom."

Her mother beamed. "That's what I told him."

"I saw the race. What happened?" Her father made an obvious attempt to change the subject.

"Fuel pump."

He nodded. "That'd do it. Tough break for Pearce."

"Yes, he didn't take it well. Felt I should have noticed in my initial teardown. But the pump was new, the housing was intact, and there were no visible signs of wear."

"You did what I would have done. What any mechanic would have done."

Her father's reassurance was welcome after Ryan's lack of confidence in her. "That's pretty much what I told him. But I got the impression he still thought it was the quality of our motor."

"Don't let him push you around, Jamie. You stand your ground." He struggled to sit up, his face flushing. "We build quality motors."

"Now, don't get overexcited, Jimmy." Her mother smoothed his blanket.

"I'm not dead and I don't intend to act like it." His voice was sharp. Frowning, he patted her hand. "Sorry. I'm a bad patient, I'm afraid."

She cupped his cheek with her hand. "Not so bad. I wouldn't have you any other way. Too easy and I'd be afraid you were dying on me."

He smiled, holding her mother's gaze. The years seemed to fade away and Jamie could easily imagine them as teens in love. Her eyes misted. What would it be like to have a love as solid, as enduring as theirs?

"Don't forget, you're stuck with me for a while."

"What can I do to help?" Jamie asked.

"I have a ladies auxiliary luncheon in two days. I'll be here with your father. Would you go in my stead?"

Jamie raised her hands. "No way. Those women would chew me up and spit me out. Before I knew it, I'd be volunteering on some board I have absolutely no interest in. It'd be a worse fiasco than when you signed me up for the Poultry Princess pageant."

"That wasn't a fiasco, honey. You won." Her mother patted her cheek. "And you were absolutely stunning in your tiara."

Jamie made a strangled sound, glancing at her father for help. He shrugged.

"How about if I stay with Daddy so you can go to the luncheon?"

"I wouldn't feel right leaving your father alone."

"He wouldn't be alone. I'd be with him. It would give us a chance to catch up."

"I've got an idea." Tom leaned in the doorway. She

hadn't noticed his arrival. "*I'll* stay with Dad and you ladies can have a mother-daughter outing."

Jamie swallowed a groan.

But her mother's face lit as if she'd been given a precious gift. She clapped her hands. "What a lovely idea. It's been ages since we've had a girls' date."

"I'd really like to spend some time with Daddy."

"We'll have plenty of time, Kitten." He squeezed her hand, his gaze earnest. "Your mother's been cooped up in the hospital—it'll be good for her to get out."

Sighing, she said, "Okay. Just the luncheon, though. No volunteering me for committees, teas, pageants or fund-raisers."

"Of course not, Honey. I wouldn't do something like that."

"You would and you did."

"You're still blaming me after all these years? You'd spent so much time hanging around the garage in grungy clothes and talking engines. I wanted you to explore your feminine side."

"I can work in a garage and still be feminine."

Her mother sniffed. "Look at you now."

Jamie glanced down at her jeans and T-shirt, both clean and presentable. "I like to be comfortable."

Daddy cleared his throat. "Susan, quit harping on the girl. She's come all this way to see me and I don't care what she wears."

"You never did understand, Jimmy. She won't find a husband if she looks like a cross between a grease monkey and a homeless person."

The barb wounded Jamie more than she cared admit. She wanted to look nice as much as the next woman.

And in the corporate world, she'd conformed to that standard. The shop was a different matter.

Her daddy's voice was firm when he said, "She's a mechanic. You need to accept her for who she is, not who you want her to be."

Hallelujah! He finally understood.

"All I've ever wanted was for her to be happy." Her mom's voice trembled and tears shone in her eyes.

Uh-oh, Mom was bringing out the big guns. Her dad turned to mush at the first hint of tears. Too bad Jamie had been too stubborn to let him see her cry, or she might be CEO of Tanner's by now.

"Would you both quit talking about me as if I'm not here." She propped her hands on her hips. "I'm an adult. I hold a good job. I pay my taxes. I don't do drugs or break laws. Can't that be enough?" Her chest constricted as she asked the question that had haunted her for years.

Can't I *be enough?*

Tom pushed away from the wall. "Actually, you don't technically hold a job. You're a contract worker."

Narrowing her eyes, Jamie wished Tom would quit taking potshots. Her voice was frosty when she said, "At least I've worked out in the real world."

"What's this about Jamie being unemployed?" Her mother's voice raised an octave. "You decided to take the buyout offer?"

"Yes, I accepted the package. The paperwork's being processed. Until then, I'm technically on vacation."

"So you're back in McGuireville permanently?" Her mother's eyes sparkled. She was probably already planning the social events she could finagle to introduce

Jamie to all sorts of *suitable* men. Then she frowned. "I never intended you to be in the shop permanently. We'll have to work something else out."

Jamie closed her eyes against the disappointment. When she opened them, she saw her mother much too clearly. "So I'm good enough to prop up the family business in an emergency, but not good enough for the long haul? Nothing has changed."

"Don't talk that way to your mother, Jamie Lynn." Jimmy struggled to sit up straighter in bed. "It's never been a question of you being qualified."

"Then what was it a question of?"

"You're upsetting your father, Jamie. We'll discuss this later."

She glanced from her mother to her father. It hurt to realize she was still on the outside looking in. The square peg to the family's round hole.

Taking a deep breath, she calmed her emotions. Her voice was even when she said, "The last thing I want to do is upset Daddy. But I won't allow myself to be railroaded a second time. We *will* discuss this later. If you'll excuse me, I've got to find an apartment with a short-term lease. Very short-term."

"That's ridiculous. You'll stay in your old room at our house," her mother said.

Jamie knew she needed some distance from her family. Otherwise, she'd fall into old habits—rolling over and playing dead instead of fighting for what should be hers. "I need a place of my own. I'll talk to you later."

"What about the luncheon?"

Leave it to her mom to gloss over the confrontation

and worry about the luncheon. Or maybe the confrontation had only been surprising for Jamie. Apparently she was the only one who hadn't accepted that she might never fit in.

CHAPTER EIGHT

JAMIE OPENED the door to her new place. "Hi, Mom, I'll just be a sec."

"That's okay, I'd like to see your apartment." There was a hint of pleading in her voice.

"Come on in. I'll give you the dime tour."

She stepped inside the doorway, glancing around. "It looks very comfortable. Amazing that you were able to move right in."

"It's furnished." She gestured to include the small living area and galley kitchen. "Besides, I didn't bring much stuff."

"Jamie, I want to apologize. I spoke without thinking the other day at the hospital. I didn't consider your feelings."

Tilting her head, Jamie absorbed her admission. It was a start. "Apology accepted. We still need to talk about a more permanent arrangement later though."

"Yes, we'll talk later." She eyed Jamie from head to toe. "Is that what you're wearing?"

"A pantsuit should be dressy enough for a luncheon. It's not a black-tie event."

Her mother inspected Jamie's cream-colored suit and flat sandals. "Things are so different from when I was a girl."

Jamie linked her arm through her mom's, trying to see things from her perspective. It was a difficult task at times. But being on the defensive didn't seem to be a good option, either. "Don't worry, these days I'm dressed very appropriately. This suit cost me a pretty penny at the designer outlet in Detroit."

Tucking a lock of hair behind Jamie's ear, Susan said, "You look beautiful, dear. Forgive me for worrying? I just want you to be happy."

Jamie wanted to believe her, but it was an old refrain.

"I know, Mom."

"I'm so looking forward to having a mother-daughter outing. I can't wait to show you off at the luncheon."

"We'd better get going."

The drive was uneventful—not much had changed in McGuireville since she'd been home briefly at Thanksgiving.

The luncheon was being held at the local tea room that doubled as a wedding chapel. Jamie suppressed a pang of regret as she walked beneath the white wicker archway laced with artificial flowers. She almost expected *Here Comes the Bride* to blare from hidden speakers, instead of the soft sounds from the unobtrusive string quartet manned by local high school students. She reminded herself that the whole bride thing apparently wasn't in the cards for her. And with her basically traditional values, that pretty much precluded children. Her biological clock protested loudly at the thought.

Glancing sideways, she was relieved to see that her mother apparently had no inkling of Jamie's interest in matrimony. Otherwise, she'd have immediately rushed outside to find eligible bachelors to parade nonstop in front of Jamie.

Would that be so bad?

Of course. Because every last suitor would be deeply disappointed that the former Poultry Princess was better at torqueing a bolt than tending to hubby, hearth and home. Hadn't her last relationship proven that?

Perspiration beaded her upper lip. "Whew. One of the things I don't miss about Arkansas is the humidity."

"You'll get used to it again, dear." Her mother ushered her to a table near the podium.

Mrs. White beamed as they approached. "Jamie, Susan, I'm so glad you were able to make it. It would have been a pity to eat in the hospital cafeteria after you'd purchased tickets for this lovely luncheon."

"Tickets, plural?"

Her mother's eyes widened innocently.

"You were awfully sure I'd attend, weren't you?" Jamie whispered.

"Hopeful. Very hopeful." The affection in her tone convinced Jamie her motives were genuine. And pretty much soothed her irritation.

They walked around the room, stopping to talk to women Jamie hadn't seen in years. Pride was evident as Susan Tanner reminded her friends Jamie was from the Detroit area and had a top engineering position with one of the big three automakers.

Jamie opened her mouth to admit the engineering job was very nearly past tense, but decided to allow her mom some leeway to preen. Many of the people with whom she'd attended high school had taken jobs in the nearby poultry processing plant because they couldn't afford college. Jamie might seem an oddity to her mother at times, but at least she had been lucky enough to see other parts of the world.

The meeting was brought to order and business discussed as lunch was served. The business portion was blessedly short.

"Jamie, you're a good girl to drop everything in Michigan to come help out your parents," Mrs. White said.

The six other older ladies at the table nodded in agreement.

Jamie explained about her division at the automaker closing. "Daddy's heart attack was scary, but I was happy to come back—the timing worked out."

"Well, I know it eases your mother and father's minds to have you at Tanner. It's wonderful to see the gals these days taking on jobs only men used to do. Southern women have the grit to do anything a man can do. Why, my mother was a Rosie-the-Riveter during World War Two. So was yours, wasn't she Susan?"

Susan Tanner nodded slowly. "You know, I almost forgot about that. She worked in a gas-mask manufacturing firm."

"See, your Jamie comes by her gumption honestly. Handed down through the generations."

Jamie touched the woman's arm. "Thank you, Mrs. White. That's lovely of you to say."

"It's the absolute truth. Women today have so many more opportunities than we had, don't they Susan?"

Her mother nodded thoughtfully.

One of the other ladies chimed in, "Especially in racing. I'm hoping that gal who races Indy cars will move into NASCAR. She's a little bitty thing, but she sure can drive."

Jamie smiled, bemused. This was the last conversation she expected to hear at a ladies auxiliary luncheon.

"Jamie's been working quite closely with the Pearce Team on some engine problems," her mother interjected.

Jamie almost choked on her hush puppies. She'd thought nothing ever changed in McGuireville, but here her mother actually sounded proud that Jamie worked under the hood.

"Oh, how exciting." Mrs. White's cheeks pinkened. "Is Ryan Pearce as handsome up close as he is on TV?"

"Um, yes, I guess he is."

"He's single, you know. Quite the catch."

Her mother frowned, opening her mouth to protest.

Jamie beat her to the punch. "It's strictly business."

"Oh. That's too bad."

Yes, it is.

Where in the heck had that come from?

Jamie was grateful when her mother changed the subject and the ladies followed. Their chatter washed over her as she tried to corral her errant thoughts.

JAMIE ENTERED the Tanner garage and felt as if she'd never left. The familiar whine of impact guns, the hammering, banging and swearing. The aroma of motor oil and solvent. It all welcomed her home.

Hal, the shop lead man, glanced up and nodded. He wiped his hands on a towel and came over.

Tall, thin and stoop-shouldered, he hadn't changed much since she'd first met him twenty years ago. He'd worked for her father that long.

"Jamie, good to see you."

"Thanks, Hal, it's good to be back."

"Tom says it's just temporary."

"We'll see." She kept her tone light.

"I've kept things going for Tom. With your dad being gone and all."

She patted his arm. "We appreciate it."

Hal looked away as if embarrassed by her gesture.

"I'm here to take the heat off my brother. He says I need to look over the purchase orders. You still have the white board showing where each engine is in the process?"

Nodding, he said, "I'll see if I can scare up those purchase orders."

Jamie didn't like the sound of that. Her father always had a binder, sorted by date. "Are they still in a binder? Because if they're on the computer now, I'm sure I can find them myself."

"The binder's more reliable. Your dad isn't big on a paperless system."

She smiled. "So he's told me. Bring what you've got and I'll poke around the computer and see what I can find. Tom's still handling all the general Tanner administration, I'm just dealing with the stuff falling strictly under the running of the shop."

He shrugged, his thin shoulders and long neck giving the impression of an underfed turkey.

"Are we on time with our orders?"

"Running about a week behind. Couldn't be helped."

"Hmm. I'd like to see a backup plan in place for such events. The whole operation shouldn't hinge so heavily on one man or woman. It makes us very vulnerable.

Leads to burnout, too." Jamie wondered if her dad had ever gotten tired of carrying the whole business on his very capable shoulders. She suspected her mother had.

She went to her father's small office off the shop. There was paper everywhere. Schematics, purchase orders, invoices. It appeared PO's and invoices were there for her father's signature. She decided to cross-reference them with the orders on the whiteboard.

Hal popped his head in the door. "Need you to sign off on those invoices so the vendors can get paid. There're a couple of suppliers threatening to revoke our credit—cash only. Jimmy always leaves paperwork till the last minute."

"Don't I know it. Which vendors? Maybe I can give them a call and explain the situation."

"Tom said he'd handle it. Thought maybe you could sign off in the meantime. Or I could, if you'll allow me the authority."

"Sure, Hal. Just let me eyeball the paperwork after you make sure the backup is attached."

"Why?" His long face got even longer.

"Procedure, you know? Checks and balances. Plus it will let me get caught up quickly."

"Why do you even want me involved then?"

"You're right. Go ahead. Get it cleared off today and we'll give the new system some thought once things are back on track."

He nodded, smiling. "You can count on me."

Jamie hoped so. "I brought back the Pearce fuel pump. After I get Dad's desk in some sort of order, I'll be in the shop taking it apart. I want to find out what happened out there Saturday night."

RYAN STRADDLED a chair outside the hauler and answered his cell. "Hello."

"This is Jamie Tanner. I just disassembled the fuel pump and thought you'd like to know what I found."

He stood. "Of course."

"It was an injector."

"Moving parts will wear—it's expected on a used part. So why did it happen with a new pump?"

"It's the same manufacturer my dad's used for years. They provide quality parts. Must be a fluke."

"Tell that to Craig Blake."

"It shouldn't have happened, Ryan, and that sucks. I've raised holy hell with the supplier. And of course, we'll credit your account to make up for the inconvenience. Even though I know nothing will make up for your disappointing finish."

Her response took the edge off his anger. He'd been ready to read her the riot act and she'd taken responsibility and offered a solution. And acknowledged that it wouldn't nearly make up for what he'd lost.

"I guess that's the best you can do."

"It is. And to say I'm sorry."

"Okay." He didn't like it, but he had to respect the way she handled it. And admit to himself that it was good to hear her voice. "I just hope to hell there are no more flukes."

JAMIE JUGGLED a salad bowl and a red velvet cake, and pushed the doorbell with her knee. It was a graceless motion at best.

Tom answered the door. "Hey, Sis, I thought you'd have your nose buried in purchase orders."

She sighed with exasperation. "You know I wouldn't miss Daddy's homecoming. Besides, Hal's been a big help. Just let me in, this stuff isn't getting any lighter."

He stepped back, holding open the door. "Of course, Your Highness."

She walked through the living room of the ranch-style home. The furnishings and art reflected the blue-and-mauve color scheme of the eighties. It was comfortingly familiar, especially after the turmoil of discovering Ryan's poor finish had been indirectly their fault.

As she ducked into the kitchen, Jamie was surprised to find her mother with her head bowed, her shoulders shaking.

"Mom, what's wrong?" Jamie dumped the food on the counter wrapping her arm around her mother's shoulders.

"Oh, Jamie, I was afraid...he'd never come home again."

"That's a natural reaction. But he's here and he'll be underfoot for plenty more years."

"Now that he's home, I'm scared." She started crying in earnest. "What if they sent him home too soon? What will I do if he has another episode?"

Her heart went out to her mother. Jamie had always assumed her mom would be strong in any circumstance, indestructible. But she was finding these days her mom was human after all.

"Shh, he'll be fine. The doctor's pleased with his progress."

Susan hiccupped. "I know it's silly. I worry about waking up in the morning to find him dead."

Jamie tried not to shudder at the image. "You look

exhausted. Do you want me to spend the night, keep an eye on Dad so you can sleep?"

Wiping her eyes, her mother smiled slightly. "No, dear. I'll be fine. I'll have to face it sooner or later anyway."

"All you have to do is ask."

"I know. You're a good daughter."

Jamie's mood lightened with her praise. "Do you need help getting supper on the table?"

"No. The chicken's ready and in the warming oven. Everything else is on the table." She bustled to the counter. "I'll just set out your salad and we'll be ready. The cake's lovely, dear."

"Thanks. I learned to bake from the best."

"You certainly did." Jamie was relieved to see a teasing sparkle in her mother's eye. "Now, if you could just cook as well as you bake…"

"Probably not going to happen, Mom."

Susan sighed. "No, I don't suppose it is. Would you ask Tom to wake your father? He's taking a catnap. And if you'll tune in the race, I'll get the chicken."

Jamie complied with her request. Grabbing the remote, she punched the on button, found the correct channel and watched the race commentary come up on the big-screen TV.

Her father shuffled into the room, his hair rumpled from sleep. All of a sudden, he looked fragile. Or maybe it was something she'd refused to see after the surgery. Weak, yes. Fragile, no. Maybe her mom had good reason to worry.

Jamie shook off the thought and went to give him a gentle hug. "Hey, Daddy, you have a good nap?"

"Yes. Sure wish I'd get my energy back, though."

"You will. It just takes time. Come on into the dining room. The pre-race commentary is starting."

Jamie sat in her customary seat, as did the rest of the family. The ritual reassured her that the family would endure the setback of her father's illness. But would they ever be as close as they'd been before Jamie had been denied her place in the family business?

Shaking her head, Jamie told herself to be grateful for what they had. Her dad was recovering and, God willing, would be around for many more years.

Daddy muted the TV while they said grace. Then the volume was turned back on for the commentary. It was like hundreds of Sunday suppers before, familiar and comfortable.

The announcer said, "Any predictions on what Ryan Pearce will do on a restrictor-plate track? He's been struggling since moving up to the Cup series."

"Pearce's got a lot of talent. And he's got the edge of maturity. If he's got a decent car under him, I predict good things."

They went on to discuss other drivers and Jamie relaxed her grip on her fork.

"What do you think of Pearce, Jamie?" Tom asked.

"He's pretty down to earth. Intense. But he has integrity."

"I meant as a driver."

Jamie's face grew warm, but she refused to let Tom know he'd scored a direct hit. "He knows what he's doing. Old school, but not overly aggressive. I think he'll do well now that we've got his ride up to par."

"You're sure it's taken care of?"

"Yes. I called him today and the car's running like a champ!"

Tom raised an eyebrow. "Extra special customer service."

Jamie's blushed deeper. "That's ridiculous." *Wasn't it?*

Her father studied her face. "She was going the extra mile just like I taught both of you."

If she hadn't been so disturbed by her reaction to her brother's teasing, her father's approval would have touched her. And silenced Tom's innuendo.

Talk turned to people she and Tom had known as kids. Her mother supplied a healthy roster of her friends who had married, along with an impressive ability to remember their children's names.

This type of news used to make her defensive; now it simply made her sad. If her mom got going full-tilt, Jamie wasn't sure her composure would hold. So she resorted to one of her childhood ploys—deflecting the attention. "Hey, Tom, didn't I hear something about you bringing in a new contract?"

"Yes, a big one." He wiped his mouth and told the story of landing the account.

She tilted her head to the side, studying her brother. He'd grown into one heck of a salesman. "You've done great, Tom."

He hesitated, as if he weren't sure of her motives. "Thanks."

She was as surprised as he. Because she wasn't sure if there was any room in the organization for her once her dad returned.

Then they'd have to make room.

Jamie didn't intend to ever give up on her dream again. She'd worked too hard, sacrificing little pieces of her self along the way. The time had come to fight for what she believed in. And she believed her place was heading up the shop at Tanner. This time no one would stop her.

The conversation once again veered away from Tanner Motors and into safer territories: local gossip, politics and weather.

When the meal was over, Jamie helped her mother clear the table and serve dessert, then took her seat on the couch.

Her dad cranked up the volume to an almost deafening level. But Jamie was still vaguely dissatisfied. She wanted to *feel* motors, fill her senses with the rumble until she could barely breathe.

Leaning forward, she shut out the rest of the world as the race started. She watched the Number 63 car make an immediate bid to thread the needle between two cars in the front row. She was barely aware of cheering as Ryan made it shoulder to shoulder with the front two vehicles.

"Jimmy, calm down." Her mother's sharp tone intruded on Jamie's concentration.

"I can't. Did you see that? Pearce has guts."

Yes, he certainly has.

They settled in for a long race. The pack was tightly grouped—almost bumper to bumper. With the restrictor plates, there wouldn't be as wide a gap between winner and loser and everyone in between.

Things got wild several times. Minor miscalculations caused major problems. But Ryan stayed ahead of each accident and fared well.

"He pits intelligently," Jimmy commented. "I've heard good things about Trey Walker, his crew chief."

"I've heard some incredible stories about his personal life." Tom grinned, apparently gaining vicarious pleasure from Trey's conquests.

Jamie shrugged. "Bill Sinclair's his car chief. He said to tell you hello, Daddy."

"Bill's a good man. Made some mistakes, but came back in a big way. I give Pearce a lot of credit for taking a chance on him."

"Bill says you're the best, too. And that, um, I take after you."

"Of course you do, Kitten."

Jamie bit her tongue. Then why hadn't she been allowed to rejoin Tanner after college and work side by side with her father? The sense of betrayal came back in a rush no matter how hard she tried to get past it.

"Oh!" Tom smacked the arm of his chair. "That had to hurt. I think my guy's out of the running."

Jamie held her breath as she focused on the replay of an accident involving four cars. Tom was right. It did look like it hurt. For the driver, the crew and everyone else with hopes for this race. Fortunately, the Number 63 car wasn't involved.

Exhaling, Jamie watched intently as Ryan continued to hold his own, going shoulder to shoulder with the front two cars. But in the last lap, one car pulled away from him.

"No, Ryan, don't let him get the lead!" she yelled.

Then the second car slowly pulled away. Ryan couldn't seem to catch him.

She shrugged off disappointment. She'd been so sure he'd win this race. "He got third."

"Not a bad run," her dad said. "It'll definitely help his point standing."

Tom shrugged. "Pearce did better than I expected. But it looked like he didn't have the *cojones* to win."

Jamie glared at Tom. "He's no wimp.

"Sounds like Jamie likes the guy." The teasing gleam in Tom's eye reminded her of the time he'd caught her kissing Robby Johnson in the sixth grade.

"Shut up!" She rummaged through her purse, removing her cell.

"Who are you calling, dear?" her mother asked.

Who *was* she calling? Ryan would be neck deep in media interviews.

"Nobody." She tossed her phone back in her purse, restless and not sure why. All she knew was that she wanted to talk to Ryan and find out firsthand about the race. Professional reasons only, she assured herself.

Tom's smirk told her she didn't fool him a bit. And she wondered when her baby brother had gotten so smart.

CHAPTER NINE

RYAN WAITED until Thursday to call Jamie. It took him that long to decide he was calling her for the right reasons. Business reasons.

"Jamie Tanner." Damn, it was good to hear her.

"Hey, it's Ryan Pearce."

"Ryan." Did he detect a note of pleasure in her voice?

"I watched the race Sunday. Congratulations on a good finish."

"It should have been a win."

"Third's still good."

"I'm not complaining. But I could have won if I'd had just a little more horsepower. With restrictor plates, they shouldn't have been able to pull away from me like that."

She hesitated. "Yes, I see what you mean."

"The team detected a miss. We pulled the carburetor and it needs to be rebuilt. The O-rings are shot."

"That's odd," she murmured.

"You're telling me."

"Nobody's going to skimp on O-rings in a carburetor meant for racing. The heat alone would fry them."

"That's exactly what happened." He rubbed the tension from his neck. "Jamie, I respect you and I respect your dad, but it really looks like this engine has too many flaws."

"How's it running with the rebuilt carburetor?"

"Like a top," he admitted. "But with everything that's happened, I don't feel I can trust this piece of equipment."

"We're looking at two isolated problems—the fuel pump and the carburetor. Parts fail. It's the nature of the beast." Ryan could almost hear the trouble she had saying that. Her dad was supposed to be a perfectionist and never would have accepted this kind of initial failure rate. But Jamie had told him how Tom had stressed how every dollar counted due to their aggressive expansion.

"Not in a brand new motor, they don't," Ryan stated.

"I've got some pressing business I need to finish up here this afternoon. But I'll fly out tomorrow and take a look at the O-rings you pulled. Then, if you're having any more troubles with the motor in qualifying, I'll swap the engines out. It'll be close getting one shipped and swapped out before the race, though."

"That's why I didn't press. I don't want to go into a race on a brand spanking new motor that my crew rushed to install. Too many things can go wrong."

"Agreed. I'll fly out to Richmond tomorrow and we'll take it from there."

"Okay. See you then."

Ryan shut his phone. Jamie hadn't committed to giving the team carte blanche to make up for the crummy motor. But she hadn't told him to take a hike, either. For some reason, the thought of seeing her again made his worries a little easier to bear.

Shaking his head, he reminded himself to focus on racing, nothing more, nothing less. Relationships were for guys who had a track record for stability over the long haul.

Jamie deserved nothing less.

QUALIFYING WAS ABOUT to start when Jamie arrived at the Richmond track. Her flight had been delayed, then she'd had problems finding a rental car. Fortunately, her pit pass was at will-call and she had no problem getting into the hauler area.

She nodded to Ryan's hauler driver.

"They're all up top." He nodded toward the roof. "Go on up. Better hurry."

"Thanks." She quelled nervous butterflies in her stomach as she climbed the stairs.

Jamie said hello to a few familiar faces and glanced around. The only empty lawn chair was next to Trey's girlfriend. Forcing a smile, she went over to the woman. "Hi, Sheila, you mind if I sit down?"

"Sure, go ahead." Her response was listless.

Jamie hoped the woman hadn't sensed her antipathy. Although, upon closer observation, Sheila wasn't looking nearly as stunning today. Her complexion was pale, except for two spots of color on her cheeks.

"Are you okay?"

Shaking her head, Sheila said, "I feel kind of sick."

"Here, let me get you some water. Maybe you're overheated."

"I've had plenty of water. I think I just need to get inside." She stood.

"Do you need help going down the stairs?"

She shook her head again, swallowing hard. "I can manage."

Jamie watched Sheila until the roof line blocked her view. Jamie tiptoed to the edge. She breathed a sigh of relief when Sheila reached the ground safely. The woman looked as if she might toss her cookies.

Then qualifying started and Jamie put Trey's girlfriend out of her mind as she found a spot near the rail with a good view.

Ryan looked great. Um, the team looked great. Oh shoot, even from here he looked pretty good in his blue and silver uniform: tall, strong, self-assured. She was beginning to understand the appeal of a racing man. But with Ryan, it was more his intensity and integrity that drew her. And the way he listened to her talk about performance technology without his eyes glazing over.

She forced herself not to go there. Ryan had dealt with her as one professional to another—and that was half the problem. He'd said he respected her abilities—the instant key to her gratitude.

A roar went up from the stands, drawing Jamie from her introspection. She jumped to her feet as Ryan took to the track for qualifying.

Please have nothing else go wrong.

The superstitious part of her feared the motor was somehow jinxed, while her engineering background told her that was hogwash.

Her uneasiness proved to be unfounded. When it was all done Ryan nabbed the pole position. Raucous cheering and high fives erupted atop the hauler. The pit area was the same.

When Ryan returned to the hauler, Jamie stayed in

the background as everyone congratulated him. Then he glanced up and saw her, grinning broadly. She watched him make his way through the throng. Reaching her side, he grasped her arms. "We did it!"

"Congratulations! Pole position!" Jamie crowed.

"Thanks. I found my line and stuck to it. And the car responded perfectly."

"I'm so glad. Looks like you might not need me after all."

"Let's hope not." He opened his mouth to say something else, but apparently changed his mind.

"What?"

"Nothing. It's not important." He wouldn't meet her gaze, as if he were somehow embarrassed. A strange response from such a self-possessed guy.

He released her arms. "I'd still like you to look at those O-rings. Might be something you'll want to bring up with your suppliers."

"Of course. If I find they're substandard, we'll implement the credit we discussed." And Tom would simply have to bite the bullet and pay.

"Sounds fair."

Silence descended, as if they had nothing left to say.

"You'll stay for the race, won't you? I'll get you a pass."

"I wouldn't miss it. I have a good feeling."

"Yeah, me too." He shifted.

"Will you have the rings for me then?"

"Yeah. Or better yet, why don't you stay to watch the Busch race tonight. We're bringing some Italian food in. Ought to be a great time."

She glanced at her watch. "I've got reports back at

the hotel I need to finish and e-mail to Tom. How about if I come by later?"

"Great. About five?"

"Perfect." Jamie grinned, looking forward to an evening of racing. And maybe looking forward to spending time with Ryan, too.

THE AROMA of garlic and cheese tantalized Jamie as she approached the hauler later that day. Excitement swirled in her stomach. She smoothed the filmy peasant blouse she'd chosen to wear. Paired with jeans, it was an appropriately casual outfit, merely a step up from her usual T-shirt. A small gold locket flirted with the hollow of her throat, the V-neckline hinted at her cleavage. Her hair fell loosely to her shoulders, no ponytail, no ball cap tonight.

Had her brother Tom been there, he probably would have accused her of dressing to impress Ryan.

He might have been right.

Jamie reminded herself professional engine technicians did *not* get involved with drivers, especially technicians working under probationary terms.

Shaking her head in disappointment, she entered the hauler. The table was laden with trays full of all sorts of Italian goodies. Lasagna, spaghetti, manicotti, ravioli, chicken parmesan. A large plastic salad bowl contained an antipasto salad and a glass bowl held a green salad.

Jamie decided to go topside and find Ryan and the rest of the crew. Just as she was leaving, the boisterous group entered the hauler. Their energy was infectious and her spirits rose. Or maybe it was just anticipation at the thought of seeing Ryan again.

"Hey, Jamie, you're here," Bill said. "Grab a plate and dig in."

"Hi, Bill. I will in a sec."

Brent and Brice both said hello, as did a few of the other guys. But she sought out Ryan at the end of the food line that formed around the table. So much for her good intentions.

"Hi, Ryan."

His eyes widened a fraction as he allowed his gaze to rove from her toes to the top of her head. "Wow, you look…nice. I mean you always look nice, but tonight you look…*nice*."

Jamie laughed, her cheeks grew warm.

"Thanks. So do you."

One of the guys jostled Ryan into her. "You're between me and food, Pearce. Move it."

She felt the warmth of Ryan's hand at the small of her back as he guided her toward the table. He reached for two paper plates and handed one to her.

"Thank you," she murmured.

They filled their plates and picked up plastic tableware and napkins.

"Drinks are in the ice chest topside."

"Okay." If she'd felt like she prepared for a date before arriving, Ryan's actions seemed to confirm it. At the very least, she seemed to be an honored guest.

Climbing carefully, she hung on to the ladder with one hand and balanced her plate with the other. Another good example of why they didn't drink at the track. Making it up and down the stairs inebriated could be downright dangerous.

Ryan nodded toward two folding chairs a little

removed from the rest. "Let's grab a couple seats, then get our sodas."

When they were seated, Jamie glanced at the horizon, noticing the pinks and golds of sunset. The scent of some sort of blossom tickled her nose. She commented, "Looks like a great evening for a race."

"Any night's a great night for a race." Ryan grinned.

"Spoken like a die-hard fan."

"I'd rather be out on the track, but watching is fun, too. No pressure and I can make all the armchair predictions I want. And later, I can point out the ways the drivers screwed up."

"Like I said, spoken like a die-hard racing fan. Other folks just don't understand."

Folks like her ex-boyfriend. What would it be like to have a relationship with someone as passionate about racing as she?

Jamie sipped her drink, glancing at Ryan from beneath her lashes.

As if sensing the direction of her thoughts, Ryan reached over and brushed his thumb against the tip of her nose. "Fizz from your soda."

She ran her tongue over her bottom lip in case she'd missed a splash.

His gaze dropped to her mouth. He seemed unable or unwilling to look away.

Jamie's heart thudded in her chest. She leaned a fraction closer, while her mind listed all the reasons this was *so* not a good idea. But instinct told her a kiss with Ryan Pearce might be worth the career ramifications.

"Ryan, Jamie, either of you seen Sheila?" Trey interrupted their moment.

Jamie leaned back in her chair, relieved, yet disappointed. “Not this evening. Is she feeling better? I think the heat got to her earlier.”

Trey glanced away. “Yeah, overheated. I better go look for her.”

Jamie caught Ryan’s gaze. “I hope everything’s okay.”

He shrugged. “I’m sure it is. Trey’s been different with Sheila. I think it’s serious.”

“He has a reputation for playing the field.”

“Yeah, but the field seems to have narrowed to one. And he’s very considerate with her.”

“Not the others?”

Ryan hesitated. “Trey treats a woman like a queen while he’s on the chase, but loses interest quickly.”

“Maybe he’s grown up.”

“Maybe. I just figured he was one of those guys like my dad. Missing the commitment gene. Unable to stick around for very long with one woman.”

Jamie was uncertain how to respond to his revelation. It made her feel good that he trusted her enough to open up. “Your dad left your mom?”

He glanced away. “When I was five. I don’t remember him much.”

“You don’t see him at all?”

He shook his head. “Nope. My mom never remarried, either. I missed out on all the father-son stuff.”

“That’s too bad.” She ached to say something terribly wise and erase the sadness in his features. But her mind went blank, so she grasped his hand and squeezed.

“What about your folks?” he asked.

“They’ve been married for thirty-seven years. Still

kiss and hold hands." Jamie glanced at their clasped hands. She released his on the pretext of picking up her plate. "I think one of the hardest parts about my dad's heart attack was his worrying about Mom."

"I've never been around that kind of marriage. I figured it was a fairy tale."

"No, it's real. Too bad Tom and I haven't been able to carry the relationship success into the next generation. Mom worries she'll never have grandkids." Jamie kept her tone light, despite a pang of wistfulness.

"You haven't been married?" he asked.

"I've had a few serious relationships. Never married though. How about you?"

"It sounds kind of worn out, but I'm married to my career. Racing at this level doesn't leave a lot of room for a personal life. A relationship has got to be rock solid to make it through the time demands, the travel, the media spotlight."

"That's a hard life. I've never thought much about the toll on a driver's family." She tucked her hair behind her ear.

"Especially the kids. I'm not sure I could pull off being a driver *and* a father."

Jamie speared a ravioli, trying to keep her expression pleasantly noncommittal. It was none of her business if Ryan passed up the opportunity of parenthood. Still, she couldn't help but comment, "You're selling yourself short. I've seen your loyalty to your friends, the way you really care. You'd make it work somehow."

"Thanks."

Resisting the urge to roll her eyes, Jamie figured she'd violated the cardinal rule of guy conversation—

never discuss anything remotely touchy-feely. *Especially with a woman.*

They ate in silence for a few moments, several conversations from nearby drifted around them. One crew member theorized that Sheila had Trey henpecked. Another debated the merits of the new car design being considered by NASCAR.

Forgetting her awkward conversation with Ryan, contentment stole over Jamie, as if she'd finally found her place in life. It was wonderful to be here with people who felt the same as she did, who understood her need to be at the track.

She glanced up to find Bill watching her. He nodded slightly, then joined in a conversation with Brice and Brent.

Trying to find less personal common ground, she asked, "How did you come to find Bill?"

"He found me. My old car chief was looking for a more prestigious team—only I didn't know. As luck would have it, Bill came by the hauler one Saturday when I was signing autographs. Gave me his business card and said if I ever found myself needing a car chief, he was the right man. Said he understood why people might have doubts about him, but he'd turned his life around and was willing to work for the first two weeks for free to prove it."

"If Bill's network is as reliable as my dad's, he probably knew the minute your car chief put out feelers."

Ryan chuckled. "That's no lie. My car chief quit two days later and I gave Bill a call. He's been rock solid ever since."

"Did he get paid for those first two weeks?"

"Hell, yes. I insisted on Craig paying him. The man does the work of two. He works smart and he means what he says."

They chatted for another hour or so. When the race was about to start, they moved to stand at the rail. Ryan's hand lingered on the small of her back. It was comfortable, yet unnerving to have him stand so close.

Ryan murmured, "Are you having fun?"

Her mind went blank. His aftershave tickled her nose, his breath tickled her ear. And in her imagination, he tickled the sensitive place on her neck.

"Oh, yes. I'm having fun." *Too much fun.*

Fortunately, Trey squeezed in at the rail, saving Jamie from having to think of a more intelligent response. But his arrival pushed Ryan hip to hip with Jamie. Awareness seeped through her, slow and seductive.

"Trey Walker, this discussion isn't over." Sheila stood behind them, arms crossed, eyes blazing.

Trey slowly turned. "I said it would have to wait for another time."

"I deserve better than this. I'm going home. If you come to your senses, you know where to find me."

"Sheila—"

But he talked to her back as she marched away. Sheila was down the stairs before he moved. Possibly that had been his intention.

"Wait," he murmured to nobody in particular. The plaintive note in his voice raised goose bumps on her arms.

It was on the tip of her tongue to tell him to go after her but she wouldn't interfere.

Trey shrugged and turned back toward the rail.

"Wanna talk about it?" Ryan asked.

"Nah. Maybe later."

Soon, Trey was his old happy-go-lucky self. Apparently Jamie was the only one who noticed the pain lurking in his eyes, because nobody called him on it.

Jamie tried to tell herself she was relieved the intimate moment with Ryan had passed. But it felt a whole lot more like disappointment and that scared her. Ryan Pearce was the last man she should consider getting involved with. She could just imagine the field day Tom would have with that kind of information.

Ignoring her conflicting emotions, she concentrated on the race. It was a good one—close, exciting, with many near-misses and one pileup.

It was nearly midnight when Jamie started saying goodbye to everyone.

"I'll walk you out to your car," Ryan offered.

"You don't need to do that." She was pleased and nervous all the same.

"Yes, I do."

Jamie shrugged.

As they walked across the parking lot he grasped her hand. A few people straggled across the parking lot, but for the most part they were alone.

Jamie knew she should probably disengage her hand, put some distance between them. Instead, she found herself gazing at the sky, where a quarter moon peeked out behind a wisp of a cloud. It felt good to connect with a man again, even this innocently.

Ryan squeezed her hand. "What're you thinking?"

"That I really shouldn't be here."

"I think this is exactly where you should be."

She stopped to study him. His face was half-shadow, half-revealed by the weak light of the moon. His jaw was strong, his eyes bright with sincerity.

She reached up and touched his jaw. "What's going on, Ryan?"

"I like being with you, like talking to you. We seem to be on the same wavelength." He hesitated.

"But?"

"But I decided a long time ago not to get involved with a woman like you while I was racing."

"What kind of woman am I?"

"One who deserves more than a quick fling. One who…tempts me to want more than I know I can have."

"I'd argue the logic with you, except you're the last guy I should be getting involved with right now."

"Why?" His voice held a touch of outrage.

She smiled at his about-face. "I have goals at Tanner. Getting involved with a driver, particularly one we do business with, will simply give my brother ammunition to say I don't represent the family business well. After all, neither he nor my dad ever had that problem."

"If there were more women drivers, maybe they would." His eyes sparked with mischief. A trait she found way too attractive.

"Possibly. I'm wondering why it should matter, since we both agree we shouldn't be more than friends?"

He shook his head. Wiping his hand across his jaw, he grinned. "You got me there."

They resumed walking. Ryan hummed under his breath. Then he stopped in his tracks. Jamie stopped, too. "What?"

He stepped closer. “There’s one thing I hate worse than being called a hypocrite.”

“What’s that?”

“Suspecting it’s the truth.” His voice was husky, his gaze roamed her face, stopping at her lips.

She opened her mouth to protest, “I didn’t call you—”

He looped his fingers through her belt loops and pulled her against him. His breath was warm on her face when he murmured, “Yes, you did. And now I need to redeem my self-respect.”

When he lowered his mouth to hers, his lips were warm and persuasive. He coaxed her mouth open, his tongue inviting hers to play. Heat stole through her. Good intentions fled. She’d almost forgotten how complete she felt in a man’s arms.

“Ryan,” she murmured against his mouth.

Groaning, he wrapped his arms around her and held her tight.

Jamie responded wholeheartedly, hoping against hope his self-respect wouldn’t be claimed at the expense of hers.

CHAPTER TEN

JAMIE'S MOUTH was sweet beneath his. Her response told him acting on his attraction had been the right thing to do.

He held her close, enjoying the feel of her body pressed to his. His imagination ripped away their clothing and he could almost feel in torturous detail how smooth her skin would be, how perfect her shape beneath his hands.

He lost himself in the sensation of exploring Jamie, her mouth, her neck, the fragrant spot behind her ear. The silky texture of her hair.

Meeting him kiss for kiss, caress for caress, she twined her arms behind his neck and snuggled closer, if that was possible…

Catcalls invaded his senses, jolting him back to reality and the realization that he was making out with Jamie in the race track parking lot.

A few fans walked by, apparently uninterested in the identity of the two love birds. Thank goodness they both were in civilian clothes. A slow day at the tabloids could make for all sorts of insinuations.

He reluctantly released her and backed a step. "Boy, that got out of hand quickly."

"Yes, it did." The tremor in her voice made him feel like a jerk.

"Look, I'm sorry. I shouldn't have started something like this."

Even as the apology rolled off his tongue, the distance between them seemed to make him want her all the more. He leaned toward her, unable to help himself.

She raised a hand. "No, Ryan. I need to think about this. So do you."

"I guess you're right."

He'd always confined his risk-taking to the track, and only took calculated risks at that. Until now. There was nothing calculated about this almost overwhelming urge to jump into a relationship without thought to consequences.

But the little boy who'd grown up without a father bore the scars of others throwing consequences to the wind. And it wasn't a place he wanted to revisit as an adult.

JAMIE SELECTED a folding chair and sat toward the edge of the hauler, waiting for the race to start. She was too nervous to sit still, but didn't want to freak out Sheila by pacing the length of the hauler.

Ryan won the pole position. On the inside, he started shoulder to shoulder with the car placing second in the qualifying. It was an excellent way to begin what could be an exciting evening.

Sheila leaned near, her tone conspiratorial. "Tell me what's *really* going on with you and Ryan."

"Nothing." Jamie started to blush.

"You two seemed chummy last night."

Changing the subject seemed to be the best course. Jamie said, "I'm glad to see you're feeling better. Sometimes the heat can sneak up on you."

Sheila glanced away. "Yes, it can. I'm much better."

Fortunately, the announcer began introducing the drivers and Jamie didn't need to try and chat with Trey's girlfriend. She put on her headphones and lost herself in the race.

She held her breath as the outside car took the lead. Ryan went high, trying to get around him, but couldn't seem to pass.

Trey's voice crackled on the headset. "What's going on? Is it slick on the high side?"

"I don't know. Car's hesitating again. It feels different."

No, not again. A horrible sense of déjà vu settled in Jamie's chest.

"It's not the carburetor. Switch to the backup box and see if that helps."

"Will do."

Jamie frowned, waiting for Ryan to switch.

Cars from behind started to press the Number 63 car and he didn't seem to be able to hold them off.

"It's not working, Trey."

"You want to come in?"

There was silence for a moment. "No. I can't afford the time."

There was silence on the airwave.

Slowly, the Number 63 car started to pull away from the pack. He was gaining on the front runners when Jamie detected a trace of smoke.

It couldn't be.

The spotter radioed Ryan to tell him the engine was smoking. There was no response.

Number 63 gained more ground. Smoke was clearly visible now.

"Let up, Ryan, let up," Trey said. "You're smoking bad."

"Then I don't have anything left to lose."

As the Number 63 car gained more ground, smoke poured from the engine.

Jamie held her breath.

Ryan slowed. His car coasted into the infield. The yellow flag came out.

Covering her face with her hands, Jamie was barely aware of the tears trickling down her cheeks. The engine was blown.

RYAN FACED the TV cameras. He took a deep breath to get hold of his emotions while an announcer stuck a mike in his face.

"This race was vital. Ryan, what're you thinking right now?"

That I'm not in the mood for this.

Instead, he calmly said, "I'm disappointed. The car was running great, we had a shot at the lead."

"Did you think about letting off at the end and saving your engine?"

"That was a consideration. But I decided to go for it." Because he hadn't had anything to lose. Except possibly his ride when the owner did the math. At seventy thousand dollars a pop, motors didn't grow on trees for small teams like his.

Ryan remembered his on-air manners and said, "Excuse me." Then he stalked off to the hauler, where he could vent in relative peace. In front of say, ten or twelve people, instead of hundreds of thousands. Two hours later, Ryan was still in no mood to talk. But talk, he did. It was part of his job. First, he'd had to participate in the post-race media wrap up.

A different announcer won his undying gratitude by not asking him obvious questions about how he felt. Instead, the guy pointed out how well Ryan had done before the engine failed and commiserated on the bad luck. His wrap-up had included an encouraging remark about what a bright future Ryan had once he got the equipment problems handled.

Ryan made a mental note to be available the next time the man wanted a feature.

Knowing he couldn't put off the inevitable butt-chewing, he headed for the hauler, where the owner, Craig Blake, waited.

Fortunately, they had the whole place to themselves, because Ryan feared the conversation would get loud. Craig was a good guy most of the time, but had a fierce temper when he felt backed into a corner.

The fiftyish millionaire didn't wait for the door to close behind Ryan before he demanded, "What the hell did you think you were doing?"

Ryan took a deep breath, willing himself to stay calm. "I was racing."

"You knew that motor was smoking and you pushed it anyway."

"Yes, sir, I did." There was no use trying to deny the truth.

Craig stepped forward, getting Ryan's face. "Do you want to share with me why?"

Ryan hoped it was a rhetorical question. But as the silence extended, he figured maybe Craig wanted an answer.

"I needed the points and I didn't have anything to lose."

"How about seventy-five thousand dollars? That's what a new motor costs."

"I realize that, sir, and I'm sorry. I made an error in judgment." One he'd probably repeat given the same set of circumstances.

Craig paced the lounge area. "You're on thin ice, Pearce. Our sponsors aren't happy. The Divine Products people are making noises about pulling their sponsorship. If they bail on us, there is no rest of the season."

"I understand. I'll do my best to see that doesn't happen."

The man's eyes narrowed. "Oh, you'll do better than that. You'll finish in the top five next week or you better find yourself another ride. With the way you've performed this season, good luck."

Ryan reminded himself that Craig's interference was generally minimal—he was strictly hands-off, leaving most of the day-to-day details to Ryan and Bill. A win would go a long way toward getting Craig off his case.

"The top five. Got it. I'll be there," he promised.

Craig headed for the door. "See that you do. Or this is the end of the line, Pearce."

Ryan exhaled slowly as Craig left. He took a few precious minutes to contain his frustration. No need to run around the garage like a raging bull. Still, he couldn't help slamming the hauler door behind him as he headed for the garage.

There were still fans and visiting corporate dignitaries milling around the infield. Several fans asked for autographs. He obliged the ones who asked nicely and seemed to understand he'd had a rotten day. The loudmouths he ignored.

By the time he reached the garage, Ryan could have easily ripped someone a new one. Taking a deep breath, he walked inside.

The engine was on a work table. Power tools whined as Jamie worked on one side, Bill on the other.

Silence descended when they saw him.

Bill stepped forward. "It's gotta be the valves."

Ryan was really tired of people pointing out the obvious. He mentally counted to ten. His voice was even when he said, "That would be my guess. Jamie, what do you think?"

"I agree."

"Good. I'm glad we have a nice little consensus. Now, I want a new engine flown immediately to our garage in North Carolina, free of charge. Jamie, I'll put you in touch with the supplier I want to use so you can set up a direct bill. After that, I'm done with Tanner Motors."

Jamie flinched, then raised her chin. "I agree you deserve a new motor. I'll make arrangements to have one expressed from our shop."

He stepped closer, treating her as he would any guy in the same situation—using the intimidation factor. "No. I don't want *anything* from Tanner. This engine was a pile of junk and the next one will be, too. I'm not taking the chance."

And she reacted as a man would. She got in his face, poking her finger in his chest. "You're out of line, Ryan. This is my father's work you're talking about. I intend to make this right, but I won't be insulted. Tanner stands for quality."

"Then how do you propose to make it right? I've got Darlington in a week. That's a hell of a track under the best conditions."

Jamie backed a step, her expression thoughtful. "We've got unacceptable part failure. Since I wasn't around until recently, I can't assure you one hundred percent that our current shop product is any different until I investigate fully. We obviously don't have time for that."

"Obviously." Ryan could feel the pressure build. The thought of driving at Darlington was enough to make his head start pounding. It had been a total nightmare when he'd raced there during the NASCAR Busch Series. Next week, the cars would be going a whole lot faster. "What miracle do you plan to perform in the next five days? And don't even bother suggesting you rebuild this motor. I don't want any more surprises."

"I'm coming to Charlotte. I'll build you a new engine from the ground up. You can choose the parts suppliers and brands. Since it's a racing town, we shouldn't have a problem finding quality parts."

He thought about it for a moment. He'd watched Jamie work—he trusted her judgment and abilities. If he chose the suppliers, it was a workable solution—not ideal, but workable. "Five days is all you get. Otherwise, if we change out the motor after qualifying, I'll have to start at the back of the pack. And I don't want something that's been slammed together."

Jamie stiffened. "I assure you, I don't slam a piece of equipment together. Time will be tight, but I can do it. You won't have a problem with an engine *I* build."

"I hope to hell you're right. Let's do it."

"Wait a minute." She held up a hand. "I'm not done yet. We haven't ruled out sabotage. I want total access to the old motor, along with the O-rings you removed from the carburetor. If I find the problems were the result of sabotage or aftermarket modifications, your team will pay for parts and labor. If it's a Tanner problem, you'll have the new engine I build free of charge."

Ryan didn't like her implication. "My crew isn't dirty."

"I didn't say they were. But I don't intend to commit myself to paying for something we might not have done."

"But—"

Bill stepped between them. "She's being fair, Ryan. Don't push it. This way maybe we don't have to involve Craig any more than we already have. He might just decide to cut his losses for the season. Tax write-offs look awfully attractive with a team failing like this. He isn't going to throw good money after bad."

Ryan crossed his arms over his chest. "You overheard my meeting with Craig?"

"I listened in. What affects you, affects us and our livelihoods. Bottom line, we don't get you fixed up with a solid car by next race, we're all gonna be out of a job."

Ryan sighed. "Where's Trey? I want to hear what he has to say."

"I saw him leave with Sheila," Brice said.

Ryan cursed under his breath. He trusted Trey like a brother, but he'd been acting strangely lately. Ryan had wanted to talk to him last night, but Trey had put him off.

"Bill, get him on his cell and tell him to get his rear back here ASAP. We need to figure some things out *fast.*"

JAMIE ONLY partially listened to Ryan and Bill make plans to drop the motor in the car and load up for Charlotte. The hauler was pressed for space as it was—the best place for the motor was in the car.

She was distracted by the missed call tone on her phone. Flipping it open, she noted it was her mother's number. *Oh no. Had her father had another heart attack?*

She tuned out the guys long enough to listen to the voice message. It didn't sound urgent and there was no indication of her dad having a relapse. Breathing a sigh of relief, she turned to Ryan and Bill.

Ryan glanced up. "Jamie, I'm not letting it out of my sight except when it's on the hauler. I'll be in the shop twenty-four/seven till we have some answers."

Great, all she needed was to have Ryan hanging over her shoulder while she was on a tight deadline. If her nerves weren't raw enough with professional pressure, memories of their kisses the night before rattled her. But first and foremost, her loyalty was to Tanner Motors.

She straightened. "That's not necessary. You know you can trust me."

"It's not that I don't trust you." His hesitation was almost imperceptible, but it spoke volumes. "Okay, so

I guess that's what it looks like. Mostly I have to be involved or I'm going to go crazy."

Jamie couldn't help but understand. His future was on the line as well as hers. "I'd be the same way. I'm one hundred percent behind you, Ryan. Don't ever doubt that."

"What if it comes down to siding with your family business or siding with me?"

"I'll side with the truth." She raised her chin.

"It might not be that clear-cut."

"You're the one borrowing trouble," she said softly.

His eyes narrowed as he whispered back, "What do you mean?"

"Are you sure you're okay with what happened last night? I wonder if you think getting close to me might jinx your chances of competing."

"That's ridiculous."

She held his gaze, willing him to be the kind of stand-up guy she'd hoped. When he didn't blink or glance away, she was satisfied. Nodding, she said to Ryan's team, "Okay, let's get things moving. It's going to be a long way to Darlington."

The guys jumped into motion.

"What's the plan folks?" Trey strolled into the garage with Sheila at his side.

At the sound of Trey's voice, Ryan turned, ready to read him the riot act. As his best friend he should have had Ryan's back when things got tough. "Where the hell have you been?"

"I took Sheila out for a late dinner."

"As crew chief, don't you think you should have stuck around to examine the engine?"

"It's blown. Needs a total teardown. Pack it up, send it home. We'll worry about it later."

Ryan could barely believe Trey's breezy attitude. "You knew how important this race was to me. You should have been here to hammer out a game plan. And you thought dinner with your girlfriend came first?"

Trey glanced at Sheila, who made all sorts of unspoken promises with her eyes. "News flash, Ry, I have a life outside racing. So sue me."

Brent and Brice gave a collective gasp.

"Don't give me that crap. You know there's very little personal life during the season. It's carved out in bits and pieces and certainly not after a catastrophe like today."

Sheila tucked her hand in Trey's. He glanced at her, held her gaze. Then nodded. "You know what? That's not good enough anymore."

"Why not? You used to eat, sleep and breathe the team."

"Exactly. You assumed I'd always be that way. But I'm making changes in my life, getting my priorities straight."

Dread settled in Ryan's gut. "Where do we fall in your priorities?"

Trey's eyes flashed with emotion. "The Pearce Team can't come first anymore. I need more balance." He wrapped his arm around Sheila. "More stability."

"How long have you felt this way?"

"A couple months."

"Why didn't you talk to me about it?" It hurt to realize his best friend had shut him out.

"Hell, Ryan, I know how dedicated you are—it's all or nothing. And you expect no less from the people who work for you."

"That's how we'll create a winning team."

"Yeah, but it gets pretty lonely. Sheila and I have been talking about it and I intended to quit at the end of the season. But things have changed...I think it's best if I quit now. Sorry, Ry."

Trey turned and walked away. Sheila trotted to keep up.

Defeat washed over Ryan as he watched his friend and respected colleague walk out the door. He wasn't sure if his team could take another loss. But he'd rather know now than be surprised later.

Glancing around the cluster of people, he asked, "Anyone else? We've got our work cut out for us to make it to Darlington. Let me know now if you don't think you can stick it out."

"Don't have to worry about me," Bill said. "I don't have a personal life."

Ryan felt a glimmer of hope at the man's nonchalance. Maybe this wasn't as big a catastrophe as he thought. He shook his head; he knew it was every bit as bad.

"Brent, Brice, how about you?"

"You can count on us, Ryan." There was a new maturity in Brent's tone.

"Brice?"

"I'm with ya."

"The rest of you guys?"

The other men nodded.

"Let's do it, then."

"What about me?" Jamie asked, crossing her arms over her chest. "Am I a part of the team or not?"

He hesitated.

She tilted her head. "I can be in Charlotte early tomorrow afternoon, after I stop in Arkansas to see my dad. I assume I won't be needed before then anyway."

He nodded stiffly, "Consider yourself part of the team."

Turning to Bill, he asked, "Can you get the guys started rounding up parts tomorrow morning? We'll need everyone pitching in to get Jamie set up with what she needs."

"Sure thing," Bill said.

"Okay. Jamie, see you tomorrow afternoon."

She grasped her duffel bag and slung it over her shoulder. "We'll kick some engine-building butt."

Ryan smiled slightly. Somehow, Jamie's confidence made his situation seem a little less grim.

CHAPTER ELEVEN

JAMIE WALKED up the drive to her parents' house, wishing she'd been able to grab more than a couple of hours of sleep. Of course Ryan called and left a message this morning while she was already in the shower. By then, she hadn't been able to go back to sleep even though she wouldn't be needed in Charlotte until tonight because of parts delays.

She knocked on the door.

Her mother answered, smiling in welcome. She hugged Jamie as if it had been months instead of days since they'd last seen each other. "Jamie Lynn, I was about to call you again. Come in, Honey."

"It was too late to call by the time I got your message last night, so I figured I'd stop by this morning. Did something happen?"

"Mrs. White called yesterday to discuss the dinner announcing this year's Poultry Princess finalists. She thought you would be the perfect person to make the announcement this evening. One of the old guard welcoming the new, telling the girls what a special honor the title is. How many doors it opens."

Jamie gulped. Thank goodness she had an ironclad reason not to attend. At least once she fudged about the timing a bit. "I would Mom, but I absolutely have to be in Charlotte tonight. I'll be gone till after the NASCAR race Saturday night."

"Oh." Her mom sighed. "That's why I never wanted you in the business. It distracts you from other things in life."

Jamie took a deep breath and tried to look at it from her mother's point of view. This dinner was probably as significant to her mother as building an engine for a NASCAR NEXTEL series Cup winner.

She gave her mother a quick hug. "I don't think the girls will miss much if I don't give them a pep talk. As I remember, Mrs. White does a pretty good job of that herself."

"You don't understand, Jamie. This is your opportunity to mould young minds. Can't you postpone your trip?"

"Mom, what I do is important, too. I'll have less than five days to build a motor from the ground up. If I don't succeed, neither will the Pearce team. Ryan might be washed up for the season, and getting a ride next season will be nearly impossible."

"There *is* more to life than racing."

The sentiment was so close to the one voiced by Trey the other night it made the hair on the back of her neck prickle. Why couldn't some people understand racing *was* life? She'd given up convincing her mom a long time ago.

"Where's Daddy? I want to check on my favorite patient."

"He's where he always is—in the recliner."

"How's he doing?"

Frowning, her mother said, “He’s doing…fine.”

“You don’t sound too sure.”

“I’ve never seen him like this. He doesn’t seem to want to do anything, see anyone. Just watches TV.”

“You’re right. That doesn’t sound like Daddy.”

“I bet seeing you will cheer him right up.”

They walked into the family room, where her father sat in his recliner. It was still a shock seeing him virtually immobilized compared to the man of action he’d once been. He might have sided with her mother in order to keep the peace, but he’d always seemed superhuman in other ways. His energy, dedication and ability to zero in on any mechanical problem.

She went over and kissed his cheek. “Hello, Daddy.”

“Hey, Kitten.”

“Mom says you’re turning into a couch potato.”

He glowered at his wife. “I’ve worked hard all these years. Surely a man can rest and recuperate from heart surgery.”

“I don’t think she begrudges you the healing time. It probably makes her happy having someone to fuss over.”

“Then why’s she badgering me about playing cards and taking a walk?”

Her mother gave him a look. “The social worker mentioned that some heart patients get depressed.”

“I’m *not* depressed.” The fire in his voice reassured Jamie. “Now, sit down. You’re blocking my view of Ginger and Mary Ann.”

Smothering a smile, she figured her mom didn’t have much to worry about. Dad was just drooling over the *Gilligan’s Island* women.

"Did you see the race yesterday?" she asked a few minutes later.

"Sure did."

"The engine in the Number 63 car blew."

Her father smacked the arm of his chair. "Damn right it blew. That Pearce kid knew he was in trouble and he still kept his foot on it. He should have made a pit stop."

Jamie tried not to smile at her father referring to Ryan as a kid. "He was desperate for a good finish."

"They all are."

Jamie hesitated. She was unsure how to broach a sensitive topic with the man who was legendary in the engine-building business. "Daddy, is there anything I should know about our shop when the Pearce motor was built?"

"What are you talking about?"

"There are an awful lot of problems with this engine. We might have to give Pearce a new motor."

"I never thought I'd see the day when my own daughter thought I was incompetent."

Jamie's cheeks grew warm. "I didn't mean anything like that. I just wondered, because I'm not familiar with all the parts manufacturers you're using…"

"So now I'm cutting corners? You ought to know me better than that."

"Daddy, I'm not accusing you of anything. I just want to make sure I have all the information I need to make a decision. I'm going to the Pearce garage in Charlotte to build a new motor from the ground up. Then I'll tear down the old motor and determine the cause of the problems. Ryan will be overseeing the teardown."

"It had nothing to do with our end." He shifted in his seat, wincing. "Don't let him push you around. I bet you'll find they made modifications that weren't kosher and won't 'fess up to it."

"I've suggested that as a possibility, but I don't see Ryan risking a suspension."

"Not all drivers know what goes on in their own shop."

"He's hands-on. Says he trusts his team implicitly. And I have to say, his instincts seem right on. They're a great group of guys."

Her father studied her face. "Pearce ran good till he blew the motor."

"Yes, he did. He's got talent."

"How about sabotage? Someone might feel threatened by him."

"It's always possible. Even Ryan admits his crew isn't with the car twenty-four hours a day. And his crew chief up and quit after the race."

Her father shifted a pillow behind his back, sitting up straighter. Some of the color had returned to his face, his eyes sparked with interest. "Trey Walker? He's young, but good. I haven't heard anything about him pulling stunts like that before."

His sources of information within the series were varied and impeccable. She'd often wondered how he managed to keep his finger on the pulse of racing without hardly ever setting foot outside Arkansas.

Jamie glanced at her watch. "I can't stay long. I need to stop by Tanner and check a few things, then I'm on my way to Charlotte."

"You've got a good head on your shoulders, Jamie

Lynn. You'll figure out what's what. Just don't let some hot shot driver pull the wool over your eyes."

"I won't, Daddy."

Kiss me senseless, maybe, but not pull the wool over my eyes.

RYAN KICKED back in his recliner, sighing with fatigue. As usual, he'd run his rear off since he'd come home. Laundry, banking, a special event at a shopping mall, a quick photo shoot for a racing magazine—all by two o'clock in the afternoon. He felt like he'd been through the wringer.

He picked up the remote and clicked on the TV. Channel surfing seemed like a waste of time when his whole career might be in the toilet. To top it off, he couldn't seem to get Jamie Tanner out of his mind. He hadn't felt this way about anyone in a long, long time.

He missed her already. He'd been tempted not to call her when there'd been a parts delay, selfishly wanting to see her as soon as possible. But he knew she needed to spend time with her dad, so he'd given her the extra time.

And now he had to wait for the hauler to arrive before he could get elbow deep in the blown engine. His inability to *do* something, anything, to prepare for Darlington made him restless.

His cell phone rang.

"Hello."

"Ryan, it's Jamie."

"Everything okay? Did you get my message?"

She cleared her throat. "Yes. Dad's recovery is progressing nicely, but he's driving my mom nuts. I just wanted to let you know I'm here in Charlotte earlier than I expected."

"There's nothing for you to do till this evening."

"I'd hoped maybe we could scrounge up what we needed to at least get started."

"Believe me, Bill's been scrounging his heart out. It's killing me sitting here on my butt when there's so much on the line. I'd have called if we could get started." He'd been tempted to call several times just to talk to her—to hear her voice—but managed to limit it to the one disappointing interaction with her voice mail.

"I know. But it was either come here this afternoon or worry that my mom might shanghai me for the Poultry Princess dinner tonight. She wanted me to extol the virtues of the pageant to a bunch of girls."

Ryan chuckled. "I can see why you chose Charlotte. Doesn't seem like your type of thing."

"Thank you. I think. If it was meant as a compliment."

Smiling, he said, "It was."

"Ryan?"

"What?"

"This is probably going to sound unusual, but can I hang out at your shop? Do you have something I could work on? I don't care what it is as long as there's internal combustion. Even if it's your lawnmower."

"You want to fix my lawnmower?" Now Ryan was intrigued. Jamie was an amazing woman.

"Anything mechanical. I've…got a lot on my mind. When I need to think, I fix things."

"Kind of helps the wheels get turning in your mind?" He leaned back in the recliner. "Frees you from all the outside stuff?"

"Exactly." She sounded relieved. "I was afraid you'd think I was weird. It used to freak out my boyfriend. We'd fight and I'd head for my workbench in the basement."

"It sounds like a very sane response to stress. Hey, I've got an idea. We have a practice motor that needs some TLC. Why don't I meet you down at the garage and give you the tour? Then, if you still want to, you can tinker with the practice engine."

"Ryan, you're a lifesaver." The gratitude in her voice made him smile.

"I'll meet you down there in, say, half an hour?" He gave her the address and driving instructions. On his way out the door, he realized he was humming. That wiped the smile right off his face. This wasn't anything serious and he wasn't making excuses to see her.

Yeah, right.

He made it to the shop in twenty minutes. She was already there, waiting in a Mustang.

He gestured toward the shop as she got out of her car. "Come on."

"I really appreciate this. It was either find something to work on or pace the hotel room."

"No explanation needed. I understand."

They walked in companionable silence.

Ryan unlocked the side door to the garage and held the door for her.

"Thanks."

Flicking on the overhead lights, he said, "This is it."

The appreciation in her eyes almost made him weak in the knees. He was only slightly disappointed that it was his garage she lusted over. If she looked at him that way, he'd probably be willing to throw away everything he'd worked for.

"Nice," she breathed, walking the perimeter. "Great use of space, top-notch equipment. Definitely on a par with Tanner."

"It'll do." But he was pleased by her compliment. "Is it true what they say? That you can't go home again?"

"Oh, you can go back. But the same stuff you left behind is waiting when you return."

"I don't doubt it." He cupped her elbow with his hand. "The practice motor is over here."

"Thanks."

He pulled back a drop cloth to reveal the engine on a work table. Then ran down the laundry list of repairs needed.

Her eyes brightened and she actually rubbed her hands together in anticipation. He'd never known a woman like her.

It was all he could do keep from reaching out to her and asking if she'd like to take up where they'd left off the other night. "Where have you been all my life?" The question slipped out before he was aware of the thought.

"I beg your pardon?"

He chuckled uncomfortably. "It's not often I meet a woman who understands total dedication to a machine."

Her nose crinkled. "Oh, I understand. Much to my mother's disappointment."

Ryan moved to the large, stacked tool box on wheels. "Help yourself. I have some thinking to do, too. You mind if I hang around?"

She shrugged. "No problem. It *is* your shop."

"Not really. It's the team's, financed by both Craig

Blake and Divine Products and their line of designer incontinence products—fancy diapers from cradle to grave."

"That sucks."

"Sometimes hearing people say I drive the diaper car gets old. But it beats the alternative—no sponsor."

"I didn't mean that. I meant feeling like you're here courtesy of someone else's deep pockets."

"I don't forget for a second that I've worked my butt off to get here. I deserve every second of it. Besides, it's not so different from you working for family."

Jamie set her duffel bag on a work bench. Removing a bundle, she unrolled a fabric tool organizer. She picked up a wrench and examined it. "Yeah, but I bet you have better job security."

"Hardly. I'm on thin ice with the owner. I could be out on my tail after the next race."

"He's invested in you. He won't get rid of you that easily."

"I'm not winning. They're saying my third place was a fluke. The sponsors are giving him grief."

"So win the next race."

"So give me a car I can win with," he challenged. "It's not as easy as people think. There's more to it than haul butt and turn left."

Jamie rolled her eyes. "I didn't say it would be easy. Nothing worthwhile ever is."

"Then making the Cup races must be really worthwhile."

"It will be, Ryan. Don't ever doubt that. You have what it takes and you'll get there." Her certainty bordered on ferocity. And somehow, it eased his worries just a bit.

They developed a quiet rhythm as they worked. Soon he was absorbed in removing parts, cleaning and replacing them. Occasionally, he went to the closet and retrieved a new part or at least something more gently used than what he replaced.

The only sound was the buzz of the fluorescent lights and the clink of wrench on metal. Ryan was thankful for the comparative silence, amazed at how Jamie's presence eased his loneliness and his doubts.

Jamie's voice drew him out of his thoughts a few minutes later. "You have any brothers and sisters?"

"Nope. Probably a good thing, too."

"Why's that?"

"It was hard enough for my mom raising one kid. Like I told you, my dad didn't stick around past my fifth birthday."

"There are days I'd consider myself fortunate to be an only child."

"Tom giving you grief? Or do you have other brothers and sisters?"

She sighed. "Just Tom. He's my kid brother, he should look up to me, right? I mean I'm eight years older. But sometimes I get the feeling he just resents the hell out of me."

"Territorial about the business?"

"Territorial about lots of stuff." She glanced up and flushed. "Sorry, I promise to be quiet. And I'm being very unprofessional complaining about Tom. One of the dangers of working with family."

"I won't repeat anything." He was curious about the Tanner dynamics. He'd always had been fascinated by normal, loving, two-parent families. "I can't imagine working with my mom. I know she loves me and all, but man, that woman can get on my nerves."

Jamie's laugh was warm. "I bet she's got nothing on my mom."

"You'd lose the bet then. My mom calls before every race to tell me she loves me and how she really wishes I'd consider becoming an insurance underwriter."

"You? An underwriter? Sorry, I don't see it."

"Thank God. I'd go crazy at a desk job. But she claims she worries about me. Then I have to go through the same old spiel—that racing is statistically safer than driving on the freeway or flying on a commercial airline."

"I wonder if all mothers feel the need to change their children in the name of love? Mine certainly does. But in the next breath she'll tell me she only wants me to be happy." Jamie made a noise of frustration. "You'd think at thirty-five I'd be past letting it get to me."

"Family has a unique way of pushing our buttons. Believe me, my mom knows all mine."

Jamie moved to his side. "Hold out your hand."

He slowly complied.

Placing a wrench in his open palm, she asked, "What do you see?"

The metal was warm from her body heat. Awareness teased his senses. "A wrench."

"Yes, a wrench. A terrific gift for a mechanic, right?"

Turning the tool over, he forced himself to focus on something besides the way the harsh beams of florescent light seemed to mellow to butter tones shining on her hair. "Right. Quality brand, lightweight but durable. Nicely balanced."

Jamie went to her tool organizer and pulled out a

length of lavender silk. "Would you need to decorate it with hair ribbons?"

"No." Not unless he got to trail the ribbon across her bare skin.

Focus, Ryan, focus.

"My father gave me this set when I was six. It was all I wanted for my birthday. My mother was appalled. Said it was no gift for a girl. But Dad refused to give in for once. Mom tied hair ribbons on each and every wrench and gave me a doll, too, with matching hair ribbons. She made a big deal if I chose to work with the wrenches over playing dolls."

Ryan returned the wrench. "Maybe she felt you weren't just rejecting dolls, but were rejecting her in a way. Don't most little girls want to grow up to be just like their mommies?"

"It wasn't anything personal. I just didn't like dolls." Her eyes darkened. "Why couldn't she just accept me the way I was?"

Her anguish made him wish he could turn back time and make everything right. But all he could do was try to be there for her. He grasped her chin with his hand. "Jamie Tanner, you are smart, talented and one heck of a mechanic. You are also a beautiful woman. You're the real deal, everything in one package. Your mother should be very proud of you."

Her eyes shimmered with emotion. "Ryan, that's the sweetest thing anyone has ever said to me."

Her gratitude touched him in a way he'd never anticipated. He fingered a strand of hair, amazed at the silky texture. "Aw, Jamie, somebody should've said it a long time ago."

Jamie's lips trembled. She reached up and tentatively touched his cheek. Her voice was husky when she said, "Ryan…"

He sensed they were at a dangerous crossroads. She had become so much more than a trusted colleague or even a friend. Ryan knew he needed to backtrack or risk losing his tenuous control. "Time for you to go to the hotel and get some sleep. You can start fresh in the morning."

"But—"

"Go." He was startled by the desperation in his voice. He sounded like a man on the edge. And in a sense, he was.

JAMIE PULLED into the Pearce shop parking lot at eight the next morning. Her eyes were gritty and her brain sluggish, despite the extra large to-go cup of coffee she cradled. But by replaying Ryan's words in her mind, she was able to convince herself today would be the day their luck changed. His confidence in her meant more than flowers and candy.

She walked into the garage, inhaling deeply. The scents, the sounds, all told her she was in the right place.

Her heart lifted at the sight of Ryan working on the practice motor. He glanced up, his gaze locking with hers. "Morning."

The one word seemed to crackle in the air between them.

"Morning." Her voice was husky. "How long did you stay last night?"

"Maybe an hour after you left."

She got the impression he'd stayed to avoid temptation. After Ryan's heartfelt declaration, the garage had seemed almost painfully intimate, as if they'd left the rest of the world behind and found a safe place where they could simply be Ryan and Jamie. No jobs, no titles, no games.

"The parts get here?" she asked.

"Enough to get you going."

"How about the hauler? Is it on schedule?"

"Yep. Ought to be here at noon, maybe a little before."

She stepped closer. "Thanks for listening last night."

Ryan shrugged. "No big deal."

"Yes, it is a big deal… It meant a lot."

"Jamie, I—"

Bill, Brice and Brent strolled in, interrupting whatever Ryan had meant to say.

Frustration welled. Her instincts told her they'd interrupted something special.

More guys straggled in, signaling business as usual in a team garage. It appeared most of the Pearce crew did double duty in the home garage and at the track.

Ryan held her gaze for a moment, as if promising to complete their conversation later.

"You talk to Trey?" Bill asked him.

"Yeah. I went behind Craig's back and offered him a few extra perks. He's still firm he's not coming back."

"That's not like Trey. There's something going on," Bill observed.

"Yeah, but if the guy won't talk, there's not much I can do. I thought we were friends."

"You tried, son. It's more than most guys would have done after he told you to go screw yourself."

Ryan's mouth tightened. He busied himself looking at the paperwork Bill handed to him.

"The hauler is on schedule. Bill, I'm gonna need you to step in and be crew chief and car chief. I'll help Jamie build the new engine."

"We can help," Brice said.

Ryan shook his head. "You guys help Bill get the car set up for Darlington."

Jamie straightened. "I can build the motor myself." It would be intense, demanding and exhausting, but feasible. Besides, it would make her nervous having Ryan looking over her shoulder. The practice engine was one thing. But they both had entirely too much riding on the race motor.

Ryan shook his head. "You wouldn't have time to eat or sleep. We need to get the hauler back on the road for Darlington by Wednesday night. Early Thursday at the very latest."

"I've worked straight through before."

"Not this time you won't. I don't want you making mistakes because you're fatigued. You or someone else could end up injured."

She opened her mouth to tell him she didn't make mistakes, but closed it. Everyone made mistakes. Even more so when tired. "I don't have a choice, do I?"

He shook his head.

"Then we'll do things my way." She softened her words with a smile. "You're there to assist me, not give orders."

"Yes, ma'am." Ryan saluted.

"We'll see how well you take direction."

"I'm better at *giving* direction. But I'll survive."

Jamie only hoped *she* did. Because she was finding Ryan had so much more heart than she'd ever imagined.

CHAPTER TWELVE

JAMIE HAD NOTICED one truth about tight deadlines; Murphy's Law reigned. And the Pearce project was no different. The hauler was delayed because of stalled traffic coming into the city. A tanker had overturned, spilling chemicals. It had taken hours for the HAZMAT crew to get the spill cleaned up. And the parts delivery truck was stopped in the same mess.

Everyone was tense and Jamie was starting to sweat. Doubts surfaced; panic wasn't far behind. Sure, she'd dabbled in the pits in Michigan, but didn't have the production experience her dad did. Was she physically strong enough to handle that kind of intense, non-stop, labor? Shaking her head, Jamie hoped all those hours in a Michigan gym would save the day.

Ryan tapped his fingers on the work bench. "They should have been here by now. The road's been open for a while."

As they lapsed into silence again, the hauler pulled into the yard. Ryan jumped up and jogged to the driver's side door. The rest of the crew followed.

The driver expertly reversed the trailer into the garage.

Jamie hung back as they unloaded the race car. The

crew had done it a million times and could probably do it with their eyes closed.

Bill set the men in motion, having them remove the engine with a hoist and place it on a worktable. "This ought to keep you occupied until the parts get here." He grinned. "You and your assistant are jumpier than a long-tailed cat in a room full of rocking chairs."

"Anything's better than sitting here waiting." She smiled with false bravado. "Don't worry, I'll keep Ryan in line."

"Be sure you do. Your daddy would never forgive me if I allowed an assistant to take advantage of you."

"My daddy raised me to hold my own." Except where family was concerned. Then, she was expected to play the helpful little woman.

"Good."

Bill and the other men set to work assessing the damage and noting the obvious repair needs. She tuned them out as they started discussing the optimum suspension adjustments for Darlington.

A calm settled over her as she started disassembling the engine.

She felt Ryan watching her intently and soon he discerned her habits and rhythm. She removed parts, placing the corresponding nuts, bolts, washers and clips in zippered sandwich bags. He cleaned parts and replaced them exactly where he'd found them.

Bill walked over, closing his cell phone. "That was the delivery service. Parts truck was rear-ended while stopped in the backup on the interstate. They're gonna have to transfer all the deliveries to a new truck. They'll be here in about an hour."

Ryan swore under his breath. Jamie was tempted to do the same.

Instead, she continued dismantling the motor—work seemed the best way to relieve agitation. They moved in a familiar rhythm, working steadily.

A few minutes later, Jamie glanced up and noticed Ryan was gone. She ignored a pang of disappointment. He'd probably gotten restless with the detail work. She wiped the sweat out of her eyes and resumed working.

The good-natured banter coming from the crew made her smile.

"Hey, Jamie, how's it going over there? I see your assistant deserted you," Bill called.

"It's going good. But I guess Ryan couldn't handle the grunt work," she responded, chuckling.

The conversation flowed around her, lulling her into an almost hypnotic state as she disassembled by rote. The guys talked about the other teams and their chances to win. Rumors of team discord. Discussion of the Talladega race. Guesses on what had caused Trey to fly off the handle.

Then her stomach growled. The aroma of food reminded her it had been a long time since her breakfast sandwich this morning.

"Come on guys, get it while it's hot." Ryan called while setting out containers of food. "Soup and sandwiches from the deli and all the fixin's."

"You might make a damn good assistant yet." Bill wiped his hands on a shop towel and went to the sink.

Jamie found a good stopping point and followed suit. Her tummy rumbled as she waited to wash her hands.

Some of the guys weren't waiting. They just wiped off the grime and dug in.

Jamie selected a thick roast beef sandwich and a cup of vegetable soup. Stick-to-the-ribs food that would sustain her through the long night ahead. She pulled up a stool to one of the workbenches and sat down.

Ryan pulled up a stool next to her. "I would have told you I was leaving, but you seemed pretty intent on what you were doing."

"I figured boredom had gotten to you."

"Yeah, the fun part is putting it back together. But I enjoy this part, too. You're very precise."

"Have to be when working with engines." Jamie bit into her sandwich. It was delicious. After swallowing, she commented, "A lot of drivers wouldn't do this."

"Work in the shop?"

"Yes. And schlep food."

"I don't compare myself to other drivers, on track or off. Besides, I figure we work more effectively when we're rested and fed. Might as well make good use of the delay." He shrugged. "It would be stupid of me to send someone else when I'm the most dispensable at the moment. Come Thursday, it'll be a different story. I won't have time to help."

Jamie's cell rang. Glancing at the display, she said, "Excuse me, I need to take this." She walked to the far side of the garage where she could hear better.

"Mom, what's going on? Is Daddy okay?"

"Still the same. He perked up a bit after your visit yesterday though. That's why I'm calling. In all the chaos, I almost forgot your father's birthday. I want to have a special family supper Thursday. I know he'll want you here."

Jamie closed her eyes. "I almost forgot, too...I can't."

"I know you're committed to solving this engine thing and I think that's commendable, but you belong at home with your family on Thursday. Surely they can spare you for one day."

"Mom, you've been in this business alongside Daddy for thirty years. You know as well as I do that it's not nine to five. I can't leave till the job's done. Not with this situation."

"You don't have to tell me how demanding the business is, Jamie Lynn. That's exactly why I never wanted you involved. Your father almost died and you can't get away long enough to attend his birthday party."

Guilt tugged at her. She wanted to be there. This birthday was all the more precious because of his brush with death. "I wish there was another way."

"Do you? Or are you obsessed with this car, this race? And then the next. What if you had children? Would you miss your child's first birthday? Dance recitals, sporting events? I know exactly how hard it is for a little girl to look into the audience and not see her daddy's face. I watched your disappointment when he wasn't there. I tried to make up for it, making a special fuss."

A pang of loss blindsided Jamie. She remembered all the events Dad had missed. Remembered how hard she tried not to appear disappointed. Apparently she'd failed.

Her voice was husky when she said, "You were great. Always there for me." No matter their differences, it was the truth.

"Your father would have been, too, if not for the demands of that business." The bitterness in her voice surprised Jamie.

"I'm sorry, Mom. I never realized how hard it was on you."

"It's always hard on the family. It was my job to keep the home fires burning. You can't expect a man to give up everything while you run off at the drop of a hat."

Jamie turned her back to gain extra privacy. "I—I'm sure there's a way to have family *and* racing. There has to be a way."

"Honey, it would take a special man and a whole lot of work. I don't like seeing you shut yourself off from opportunities."

"Who knows, maybe I'll meet someone who loves racing as much as I do." *Someone like Ryan.*

"And who takes care of the children? I don't want my grandchildren raised by a nanny."

This conversation was getting way out of hand. "Mom, we can discuss this later." Or never, if she was very lucky. "I've got to go, but I'll try my best to make Daddy's party. It'll be close, but I think I can do it."

Sure, if she sprouted eight arms and there were no more delays.

"See you on Thursday," her mother said.

Jamie returned to her lunch but her enjoyment was gone. Her mother had given her too much to think about. Somehow, it suddenly seemed real what she might be giving up if she became a top engine tech.

Ryan seemed to sense her preoccupation and didn't try to engage her in much conversation. When lunch was finished, Brice and Brent volunteered to clean up. Jamie had a hard time getting centered after the phone call from her mother.

While disassembling the engine, her mind turned

over the puzzle that was her family. She'd seen another side to her mother. Wanting to spare her daughter pain, rather than refusing to see Jamie for what she was.

"You're doing it again?"

"Hmm?" She glanced up to see Ryan staring at her. "Doing what?"

"Frowning and sighing."

"I do *not* sigh."

"Yes, you do. Like this." He demonstrated, releasing a long breath. "Is it the motor? Or is it something else?"

Jamie released her breath slowly, careful not to sigh. "For someone who professes to work silently, you ask a lot of questions."

"I'm trying to figure out what makes you tick."

She tilted her head. "Why's that?"

"I'd like to think you and I have become friends."

That was an understatement. Friends certainly didn't kiss the way they had. At least none of the friends she knew. "Yes, friends."

"Want to talk about the phone call that upset you?"

"Mom and her expectations. She wants me home Thursday night for Dad's birthday supper."

He said, "Sorry, but it doesn't look like it'll happen, barring a miracle."

"That's pretty much what I told her. The thing is, she admitted the crazy schedule is one of the reasons she never wanted me to be in the engine-building business. I always thought it was because there was something wrong with me."

Ryan held her gaze. "There's absolutely nothing wrong with you."

"I thought she saw me as some freak, consumed by

cars instead of clothes. I figured parading me around a beauty contest was her way of fixing me. But maybe it was her way of giving me an alternative to a lifestyle she thought would make me unhappy."

"Sounds like you might be onto something." He hesitated. "Racing is demanding, hard on families even during the best of circumstances. And as my mother occasionally reminds me, my genetic deck is kind of stacked against being a good husband."

Jamie wondered if he was trying to warn her away. "Because of your father?"

He nodded.

"She didn't give herself much credit for raising you right, did she? I'd be willing to bet loyalty and perseverance were two of the things she demonstrated as a single mom."

"I guess I never looked at it that way." Ryan hesitated. "All I saw was her bitterness."

Jamie's heart went out to him. He had so much to offer, yet he didn't seem to realize it. She wondered what had caused his mother to be so negative. Her mother had always been behind her—in everything but her desire to be a technician. Down deep, she understood her mom had done her best as a parent. Maybe it was time she cut her a little slack.

The new insight prompted Jamie to view Ryan's mother less harshly than she might have otherwise. "Your mother must've been hurt badly," she observed.

"Yes and it was a hard life. I think bitterness was all that got her through the day and kept her from giving up."

"A survival skill of sorts."

"Yep. So I decided to concentrate on my racing. Maybe later I can figure out the other stuff."

He gathered parts and carried them to the solvent tank. "I'll let these soak for a couple minutes while I call the delivery service again."

A shout from one of the guys stopped him. The delivery truck had arrived.

Jamie rolled her shoulders to work out the kinks. Her job had just begun.

She helped the guys unload parts and started arranging them in a logical sequence to start assembly. Ryan was right beside her. They worked much as they had before but this time building instead of tearing apart. There was a creativity few people would understand.

Losing all track of time, Jamie was surprised when she saw Ryan glance at the large, industrial-style clock on the wall and announce, "Almost midnight. Looks like we can wrap it up for the night."

Jamie looked around. "When did everyone leave?"

"Around eleven. Bill said goodnight. I thought you heard him."

She shrugged her shoulders, feeling the stiffness. Her back ached, her legs ached, even her fingers ached.

Ryan's eyes were shadowed, his jaw stubbled. He had to be just as exhausted. Jamie said, "You've gone way above the call of duty. How about if I clean the tools and put them away? I can lock up on my way out."

"Fair's fair. I'll assist and we can both get out of here."

She smiled. "Bill's right. You're a great assistant."

"Don't get used to it. I prefer the driver's seat."

"I wouldn't dream of it."

Jamie watched him clean and put away his tools in the Pearce toolbox. He was an intense guy, giving total concentration, whether on the track or listening to her.

"Let's go," Ryan said, his hand on her elbow as he guided her to the door, turning out lights as they went. After locking the door, he walked her to her car.

She was surprised when he didn't hop into the compact SUV parked next to her rental car.

"This isn't yours?" she asked. Though the Betty Boop air freshener hanging from the rearview mirror should have been a dead giveaway.

"Nope. My truck's over there."

"Whose is it? I thought everyone else left?"

"Probably someone who broke down. We get 'em all the time. If it's still here tomorrow, I'll have it towed."

She got into her car and started the engine.

Ryan watched her through the glass, his expression unreadable.

Jamie found the button to lower the window. "Something wrong?"

He shook his head. "Nah. We did some good work tonight. Thanks." Then he strode over to his pickup and got in.

Jamie smiled. In his understated way, Ryan had just paid her a huge compliment. Way better than telling her she was beautiful.

CHAPTER THIRTEEN

RYAN ARRIVED at the shop at seven the next morning. He noticed Bill pull into the parking lot behind him, followed by Jamie's rental car. His team was the best. *Jamie* was the best.

He allowed himself to detour right around that thought. He needed to be on task and so did everyone else if they were to pull everything together for qualifying at Darlington on Friday.

"Morning, Ryan."

"Morning, Bill."

They waited for Jamie, then Ryan unlocked the door.

Bill cursed loudly.

Ryan entered the bay and stopped. The place looked like the aftereffects of a natural disaster—work benches had been overturned, parts scattered and papers pulled from the file cabinets and strewn over the floor.

"Ryan, over here," Jamie's voice vibrated with pain. "We'll have to teardown and make sure nothing was damaged."

He knelt on the ground by the portion of the new engine they'd assembled the night before. "Doesn't look like anything's missing."

"We're not as fortunate with the other motor." Jamie

pointed to the engine block on the ground near an overturned workbench. Plastic sandwich bags were torn open and hardware scattered everywhere.

"The carburetor's gone." Her mouth formed a grim line. "And a few other items that could be sold quickly."

"Who would do something like this?" he asked. "Why?"

"The practice engine's trashed, too," Bill reported. "You think it's kids looking to make a quick buck?"

Anger tightened his gut. "You'd think they'd have taken tools. Or the new motor."

"Too much trouble—the tool boxes are all locked. They were probably looking for easy stuff to grab." Bill paced, emanating coiled tension. "Whoever it is, they better hope the cops find them before I do."

Jamie knelt next to Ryan and touched his arm. "I'm so sorry, Ryan. This is so unfair."

"I *have* to have that new motor for Darlington. I'm down in points and if I don't make some up there, I'm out of the Chase."

"I'm not sure we can be ready for Darlington." Bill's voice held a note of defeat. "Bad enough we're down a crew chief. Now this."

"We'll manage somehow." What other choice did they have. "We've got to call the police first, then call Craig."

Jamie stood. "I'll start checking to make sure nothing was tweaked when the motor landed on the floor. We can do it, Ryan."

"Yes, we can and we will." He rose and squeezed her arm encouragingly.

Turning, he said, "Bill, you call the police and then

help me get the practice motor and the Tanner motor sorted out." He shook his head. Despite his brave words to Jamie, he feared they couldn't recover quickly enough. But he wasn't about to admit defeat until he'd given it his all.

"Do you think it's sabotage?" Jamie asked.

"Looks like it. Trey always said we needed to be tighter on security."

She frowned. "I know he's your friend, but you don't suppose…?"

"No. He wouldn't do something like this."

"I mean the way he quit without notice?"

Ryan ran his hand through his hair. "I'm still ticked at him for walking out on the team, but I just don't think he'd do something this low."

Bill walked over and handed Ryan a sheet of scratch paper. "Here's the initial police report number. They'll send someone out of investigate shortly. They're gonna try to lift fingerprints and want everything left undisturbed. Told 'em we couldn't do that."

"We can leave everything alone but the new motor. We can't afford to lose any more time on it."

"That'll have to be good enough. I imagine they'll have their hands full fingerprinting the rest of the stuff. Oh and the officer said they'll want us to pull the security tape."

"Sure. You know more about that than I do."

"It was Trey's baby, but I can eject the tape."

"I'm going to get started." Jamie didn't wait to see if he agreed. She simply rolled up her sleeves and dug in. She wasn't even technically a part of the team, yet she intended to give them her all.

She was a special woman, no doubt about it.

He refused to contemplate the ways in which she brightened his day. Instead, he watched her as one professional gauging another.

Jamie stepped around the lab technicians, getting her tools set up. Soon, her concentration was so great he doubted she even remembered the technicians were there. Ryan watched as she inspected the motor, making notes in the small, spiral notebook she'd removed from her tool kit.

Finally, when he couldn't stand the suspense anymore, he asked, "How bad is it?"

"We got off pretty lucky. Only a few parts were damaged." She handed him the list.

He quickly read it. "Hey, Bill," he hollered.

Bill jogged over from where he'd been conferring with one of the lab guys. "What's up?"

"Jamie's got some parts she needs ASAP. Get on the phone and see what you can find. We need them five minutes ago."

"We special ordered that one." Bill pointed to the list. "It was one of the parts that got held up in the delivery delay. I can tell you right now we won't have it till tomorrow."

Defeat washed over Ryan. "Great, that's the way my luck's been running."

Jamie stepped forward, wiping her hands on a shop towel. "Have them fly it out. Buy a seat for it on the plane if you have to."

"Who's gonna pay for the flight?" Bill asked.

"I will," Ryan snapped. Removing his wallet from his back pocket, he selected a card. "There should be enough credit on this card. Tell them someone will pick up the package at the airport."

"Any particular airline? You want frequent flyer miles?" Humor brightened Bill's eyes.

Heartened by a solution, Ryan slapped him on the back, saying, "Damn straight I want frequent flyer miles. And the bag of pretzels, too."

No matter how tense it got in the shop or on the track, Bill always seemed able to defuse the situation. Come to think of it, he'd make a fantastic crew chief. Ryan made a mental note to talk to Craig about it.

"Your insurance might pick up the expense," Jamie commented.

"Let's hope so. A package of pretzels isn't going to feed me too long."

"And here I thought drivers made the big bucks."

"When they're winning, they do. And if they've got an owner with deep pockets, even when they're not winning. But our team is definitely low budget. There's a lot of other stuff that's come out of my pocket, too."

"Be sure to renegotiate that when you hit your winning streak."

He grinned. "I like your attitude. I fully intend to. Now, show me what we can work on till the parts get here."

JAMIE'S EYES were starting to cross about seven in the evening when Ryan called out across the shop. "Hey, I'm going to the Burger Barn. Anyone want to come with me? Divine Products is paying."

Jamie twisted at the waist, trying to loosen her back muscles. Her shoulder popped. "Sure, I'll go. But I'll pay for my own."

"No way. You wanted to be part of the team and eating with diaper money is part of the deal."

"Okay."

"Anyone else?"

Brice said, "I'll—"

Bill elbowed him. "You stay here. We've got too much work to do. Jamie and Ryan can bring something back."

"Oh, yeah."

Jamie got the impression she was being set up. But Bill made for a very unlikely matchmaker, so she chose to take his statement at face value.

She followed Ryan out the door. "You want me to drive?"

"Heck, no. This is my town. I drive in Charlotte."

"Just don't show off, okay? I'm not wild about letting someone else do the driving, either."

"I don't show off."

"I bet."

She was surprised to find he'd been telling the truth. He almost stayed within the speed limit and didn't weave in and out of traffic.

Ryan's hand was warm on her back as he guided her into the restaurant.

She inhaled the aroma of prime beef roasted over charcoal. "It smells heavenly."

"Go ahead and order. I'll place a to-go order for everyone else just before we leave."

"You sure we shouldn't get ours to-go?"

"Why? The parts won't arrive at the airport till ten. We've done about all we can for now."

"True." Jamie allowed herself to relax and enjoy

Ryan's company and a good meal. Soon enough, they'd be working straight through. It might be her last break until the job was complete.

They sat at a booth near the back.

Jamie bit into her jumbo deluxe cheeseburger and smiled. "This is fabulous."

"Thought you'd like it. Since you're in your working eat-like-a-truck-driver mode."

"I didn't realize how hungry I was."

"Me, neither. But I knew we needed a break."

They ate in companionable silence. Strange to think they'd only met weeks ago.

"I have to admit, I didn't think the mechanical problems we've been experiencing were due to sabotage. But now I have to wonder." His eyes were shadowed.

"Because of the break-in?"

"Yes. Turns out, only a few items were taken, possibly to make it look like theft. The whole thing just set us back time-wise. If we weren't buying that part a seat on a jet, we wouldn't have a prayer."

Jamie hesitated. She should jump right on board with his line of reasoning. It would certainly be better for Tanner Motors and her. But now she was the uneasy one. "It's starting to look more of a possibility… But I don't want to jump to any conclusions. One thing's for sure, I have no intention of leaving that motor unattended."

"Neither do I. I'd planned to hang around anyway to keep an eye on things, but now I'm positive." Ryan ran his hand through his hair. "The cops were looking at the surveillance tape when I left. They didn't seem too hopeful we'd find anything useful. Said our system has too many blind spots with no coverage."

"Whoever it was didn't seem too swift. Maybe they slipped up and got filmed."

"We can only hope." He swabbed his French fry through the ketchup.

She touched his hand. "What are you going to do for sleep? You can't work twenty-four/seven and expect to race Saturday night."

"There are a couple cots in the storage room. I'll drag them out. We can take turns getting cat naps."

"I won't be able to sleep."

"You'll have to. I need you sharp and alert."

Her mind focused on the *I need you* part and ignored the rest. It might be nice to be needed by Ryan on a personal level, in addition to the professional level. Their kisses seemed so long ago, though it had only been days. Sometimes, she wondered if she'd dreamed the whole thing.

"I hope you don't think Bill stepped over a line tonight," he said.

"Bill's great. He reminds me of Dad."

"He seems to think…you and I make a great team." His voice was low. "There are times I think the same thing."

Jamie's heart skipped a beat. "What are you saying?"

"Never mind. Just forget I said anything."

"You can't just toss out a statement like that and tell me to forget it. We agreed getting involved right now wouldn't be a good idea." She studied her plate, unsure how to proceed. "But I won't be working for your team forever."

"That was my thought. Maybe we could go out sometime when this is all done. It doesn't have to be anything serious or even romantic. Just hang out together."

Her instinct was to pin him down on what hanging out together entailed. But she told herself to play it cool. No need to define something that might or might not come to pass.

"I'd like that." *I think.*

"Good."

She found his wide smile of relief totally endearing. And knew she'd be tempted to agree to just about any kind of hanging out he had on his mind. And would probably thoroughly enjoy it.

Returning his smile, she knew she was in serious trouble. The reputation of Tanner Motors and her very career was on the line yet all she wanted to do was gaze into Ryan's eyes and exchange goofy smiles, a thought so uncharacteristic it nearly made her wince.

He grasped her hand, rubbing his thumb along her palm. The scrape of his calluses sent a sizzling invitation to all parts of her body.

If that was what he could do simply holding her hand, imagine what he could do with more intimate contact. Jamie's mouth went dry and her thoughts grew chaotic, as if her brain cells were firing at random, chanting for her to follow up that train of thought.

She concentrated hard, taming the jumble of cues. Tanner Motors. Career. Future.

"Hey, we should probably get back." Before she was tempted to find out if her memory of his incredible kisses was accurate.

"You're right." He withdrew his hand. "We've got our job cut out for us getting this motor thrown together...I'll go place the to-go order."

"To-go order. Yes." Jamie hoped her lust-induced amnesia was temporary. Otherwise, she might forget everything but her attraction to Ryan.

CHAPTER FOURTEEN

THE RIDE BACK to the garage was quiet. Ryan was out of his element and not sure how to right things. With Jamie, he wanted to be a regular guy and see where the relationship took them. But he wasn't a regular guy.

When they arrived back at the shop, he called out, "Food's here."

The guys crowded him, jostling for their meals.

Jamie laughed and moved out of the way. "You're on your own."

"Thanks, throw me to the wolves."

"Any time."

"Glad you're back, Ryan. The flight'll touch down in about forty-five minutes. You want me to have it couriered over?"

He set the food on a bench. "No, I'm on my way."

Bill nodded. "We're not going to be able to get this car together till late Thursday or early Friday, making it really tight for qualifying. Jamie's good, but I don't see anyone building a motor any sooner than that."

"I'll set those cots up in the office and then leave for the airport."

Bill's phone rang. He spoke briefly and hung up. "That was the cop. I told him we'd be here a while, so a detective's going to swing by with the surveillance tape. There are two men who arrived separately on the tape after we left. He wants us to see if we recognize either of them."

Ryan was torn. He really wanted to find the person who had wreaked havoc in his shop, but his priority was getting the car ready for qualifying on Friday. "You know everyone as well as I do. You mind handling it while I'm at the airport?"

"No problem."

Ryan was uneasy, but didn't want to entrust the part to anyone else.

He made it to the airport and back in record time.

He knew something was wrong the minute he stepped into the shop. The guys avoided his gaze. Jamie frowned. And Bill simply jerked his head in the direction of the office.

He set the box on the table where Jamie was building the motor and followed Bill. What else could have possibly gone wrong?

When Bill closed the door behind them, he knew it was something bad.

"What's going on?"

"Want you to look at something." Bill hit the play button on the VCR. It was the view from atop the garage roof where the camera pointed down on the back door.

A man approached the door, his Pearce team hat shielding his face from the camera. His steps were unhurried, relaxed almost. He pulled a key from his pocket and when he opened the door he pulled off his cap to wipe his brow.

"Trey," Ryan murmured. His stomach clenched at the

apparent betrayal. "But he wouldn't do something like this."

"I didn't think so, either. But he's been acting awfully strange lately. Then up and quitting. And he was around every time there was a mechanical problem. He could be sabotaging for another team."

Ryan sucked in a breath. "He was my crew chief—he had a legitimate reason for being here each time we had problems. But I'll be interested to see which team he signs with. There are a few who might consider something like that. I'm not much a threat to anyone with the way I've been running though."

"But you were definitely competition for the big boys when this bad luck started. Maybe your luck's had some help along the way?"

His best friend? He didn't want to consider it. Except that would mean there was a tangible reason for his problems. If he knew what he was up against, he could handle it.

"The cops said there were two men?"

"Yep. Let me fast forward to the next one."

"Think they're working together?"

"Hard to say."

Bill pressed the fast-forward button. Then another figure appeared on the screen. He rewound the tape a bit and restarted it.

This person kept his hat low over his eyes and never looked toward the camera. As a matter of fact, he held up a duffel bag to shield his face even further. When he came out a half hour later, his duffel bag bulged and he carried it low.

"Looks like this is probably our guy. Did Trey leave the door open for him?"

"Can't tell."

Ryan ran a hand through his hair. "I don't want to get sidetracked with this before Darlington."

"Don't need to worry. I've told the detective who Trey is. You have any idea who the other guy is?"

"No idea. I want to talk to Trey about this, but not tonight. You think you can get him to come by tomorrow?"

"I'll try. You know he's gone incommunicado over that Sheila woman."

"Yeah. Try anyway."

"Will do, boss."

"Good. Now I need to help Jamie. How's the setup coming?"

"Exactly as we planned. Get a strong motor in there and you'll be leading the pack."

"Good, that's what I want to hear. Now, it's time for Jamie to show what she's made of."

Bill hesitated. "Ryan?"

"Yeah?"

"I like her. She's got a good heart."

That was an understatement. "What does that have to do with all this?"

Bill shifted, then held Ryan's gaze. "I screwed things up with my own kids, so I kinda feel like you're my son. I had a woman with a good heart but I didn't appreciate her till it was too late."

"Okay. Duly noted."

"I hope so. Someone ought to learn from my mistakes. Don't let that gal get away."

Ryan rubbed his temple, where a tension headache

was forming. "Bill, Darlington comes first before I can begin to think of anything else."

Bill smiled. "I know you can attend to more than one thing at a time. Shoot, your daddy was a master at it."

Ryan stopped short. "You never mentioned knowing my dad."

"You never asked. He was all flash and sizzle, not up to the long haul."

"So my mother tells me." Ryan avoided Bill's eyes, sure that stark need was written all over his face.

"Does she also tell you your daddy was determined? He was one of the most determined men I've ever seen."

"No, we don't talk about him much."

"He was headed for the big time. Something got in between him and his dream."

"It certainly wasn't his family."

"No, it wasn't. Your daddy got too full of himself. Family is what keeps us grounded during the good times and the bad. It doesn't have to take away from your career, son. The love of a good woman can make things even better."

The room felt as if it was closing in. Suddenly, he didn't want to hear any more about his dad. All he wanted was escape. "I'm going to go see how Jamie's doing with that part."

Bill nodded. "I spoke my piece. The rest is up to you."

"Thanks." Only Ryan wasn't sure why he thanked him. Except because the man simply cared.

When he rejoined Jamie, his expression had to have been grim. Between Trey's betrayal and Bill's suggestions, he felt like his life was spinning out of control.

"What happened?" she asked, her gaze warm and concerned.

He glanced around. "I don't want to talk about it here."

"Is it about Trey? If so, everyone already knows he was on that tape."

"I'd hoped the grapevine was slower than usual. Apparently not."

She touched his arm. "They're interested. Partly because it's their livelihood wrapped up in yours, but also because they care, Ryan. They care about this little family you've succeeded in making out of a bunch of unrelated individuals. And they care about you."

His throat got all scratchy. He wondered if she and Bill compared notes.

He cleared his throat. "That's a good thing, I guess."

"Very good. It's what sets you apart from some of the other drivers. And it means your crew will go the extra mile for you. *I'll* go the extra mile for you."

Her eyes darkened with a hidden meaning that he would have loved to explore. If it were a different time and place, that is.

Her cheeks flushed, then she lowered her gaze. "Do you think Trey had anything to do with your recent problems?"

"In here," he tapped on his chest, "I know Trey would never betray me like that. But I also know he shouldn't have been here last night and it worries me."

"Innocent until proven guilty." She squeezed his arm. "You're a good guy, Ryan Pearce."

He swallowed the lump in his throat. If only she knew he simply couldn't face another loss. Trying to regain his equilibrium, he fell back on what he knew—racing. "Don't you think you should get back to the motor?"

She withdrew her hand from his arm. "Yes I should."

"We're gonna leave. Be sure to lock up, boss," Bill called from across the work bay.

Ryan glanced at his watch. Almost midnight already. "Sure thing. See you bright and early tomorrow morning."

"Always."

The shop was eerily quiet after everyone else left.

"Why don't you go in the office and catch a nap? You'll be no good driving in Darlington if you don't rest."

He didn't want to admit she had a point. He would have preferred to at least give the impression of being a hero. "Just a few minutes. But I'm staying out here." Ryan jerked his head in the direction of the cot in the corner.

"It'll be noisy. I don't use the impact much, but when I need it I don't want to worry about waking you."

"Don't worry. The sound of air tools is music to my ears. Wake me up in a couple hours and I'll spell you." He didn't add that he wanted to make sure she stayed safe. Until they knew what they were up against, he didn't want to leave her alone in the garage.

She shrugged. "Have it your way."

And he did. His feet hung over the end of the cot. Pulling the blanket up under his chin, he closed his eyes, doubting he'd sleep despite what he'd told Jamie.

His breathing deepened. He heard the clank of metal against metal as Jamie worked. It made him smile. *She* made him smile.

As he drifted off, he realized he was back at one of

the small dirt tracks his dad had frequented. He was outside their small, battered motor home, throwing a ball up in the air and catching it.

He heard tense voices come through the open window. Hushed but intense.

"Why can't you be a real father to Ryan?" his mother hissed.

"I am a real father. I keep a roof over his head, put food on the table."

"He needs more than that. Just today, he asked you to play catch and you ignored him."

Ryan looked down at his sneakers, uncomfortable that his parents were fighting about him. Kicking a stone, he wished he hadn't bugged his dad.

A knot formed in his chest. He had to make it better. Tell his dad it was okay, he didn't want to play catch anyway. It didn't matter if the guys said he threw like a girl.

But he didn't get the chance. The door flew open, banging against the side of the trailer.

"Dad," he called.

But his father didn't seem to hear. He called louder. His dad stalked away, his mouth a hard angry line.

Ryan knew he'd done something very, very bad. He'd made his father mad. From inside the trailer, he could hear his mother crying softly.

He raced after his father to say he was sorry. But his dad was already in his souped-up Camaro, tires spewing gravel as he swerved out of the parking lot.

When his father didn't return that night, the tightness in Ryan's chest grew. It felt like a big old scary monster sat on his chest.

The next day, his mother took him aside and explained his daddy wasn't coming back.

JAMIE STIFLED a yawn. Her vision was beginning to blur. Her motions were slow. In a perfect world, she'd go back to the motel and sleep for at least eight hours. Then, come back refreshed in the morning.

But she didn't have the time. She would have to keep pushing through the fatigue.

She put a little more torque behind her wrench than she intended and almost stripped the bolt. "Watch it, Jamie," she whispered. Now wasn't the time for careless mistakes.

"How's the motor coming?" Ryan's voice was husky with sleep.

She glanced up and smiled. Sitting on the edge of the cot, he looked like a little kid awakened from a nap. His hair was mussed, he knuckled the sleep from his eyes. But his shadowed jaw was all man, as was the way his T-shirt hugged his muscular chest. He looked entirely too good and she was fatigued and vulnerable. All she wanted to do was to snuggle into his arms and never leave.

"I need to take a break. I'm going to take a walk, clear my head." And how!

"I'll come with you."

"No. That's sweet, but I can take care of myself."

Ryan stood, hiding a yawn behind his fist. "Be careful and stay close to the shop. I thought the security around here was pretty good before the break-in. I'd hate it if anything happened to you."

His concern touched her. Sometimes she put on such

a good front of being independent that people forgot she might be vulnerable. Her voice was husky when she murmured, "Thanks, Ryan."

Jamie glanced over her shoulder when she reached the door, catching Ryan as he watched her. Concern and longing were evident before he could hide his expression.

Her heart did a little dance. She walked out the doors into the perfect night, raising her face to the star-studded sky. Charlotte in May was a wonderful place. The evenings cooled off enough that she could walk comfortably.

Jamie emptied her mind as she strolled through the small industrial park. Scattered security lights broke up the shadows, lighting her way.

When she returned to the shop, her head was clearer and the underlying fatigue nearly gone.

She found Ryan examining the motor.

"What do you think?"

"You've really cranked on this one. If I didn't know you better, I might worry about quality."

"Thanks for the vote of confidence." His backhanded compliment nagged at her. Because it reminded her of the very thing she'd thought about her father and the other motor. That if she hadn't known her dad better, she would have worried that he'd somehow lost his edge or cut corners.

"What can I help with?" Ryan asked.

"Nothing. I'm getting to the point where I want to work alone. You'll only distract me."

He grinned. "Hey, at another time, I might enjoy distracting you."

The mischief in his eyes made her heart thud.

"At another time, I might welcome the distraction." The admission was out before she could stop it.

Ryan rubbed his thumb across her cheek. "Grease."

Fatigue addled her brain, coaxing her to lean closer. To raise her face, invite his kiss.

CHAPTER FIFTEEN

RYAN HELD his breath.

Jamie was so beautiful. But the vulnerability in her expression caught him off guard.

Calling himself every kind of fool, he kissed her anyway.

She sighed against his mouth, her lips warm and giving. His body clamored to deepen the kiss, take the contact to a much more intimate level. But he held tight to his control.

Gently moving his mouth against hers, he explored.

She settled against him, resting her palms against his chest. The gesture reminded him there were boundaries he shouldn't cross again. Both professionally and personally. No matter how tempting.

Thought flew out the window when she snuggled close. Full body contact was something he sorely missed after months of self-imposed abstinence. But it was more than just sexual need. He could imagine waking up next to her and discussing the pros and cons of restrictor-plate racing.

Ryan pulled her closer, the warmth of her body reminding him just how long it had been. And how very, very, sweet it would be to lie naked with her, exploring every inch of her body.

He deepened the kiss. Their tongues twined, his pulse pounded. He wanted this woman, right here, right now.

Then she pulled away from him, her breathing shallow.

He reached for her but stopped. She was doing the right thing to put on the brakes. Someday he would appreciate it.

But right now, his body screamed in frustration.

THE NEED IN RYAN'S EYES warmed Jamie to the soles of her feet. Hope bubbled up inside her, encouraging her to believe in the impossible. Ryan sure looked like a man falling for a woman. And she sure was falling for him.

Love?

Jamie refused to go there. She couldn't possibly be falling in love with a man she'd only known a few weeks.

She cleared her throat. "That probably wasn't a good idea."

"But fun." A glint of mischief lurked in his eyes.

Where was the guy determined to race at the expense of all else, including having a relationship and everything that went with it?

"We need to stay focused. We've both got a lot on the line. Maybe later we can explore this attraction..."

The light faded from his eyes. "I'll hold you to it."

"You've got to realize how difficult a position this puts me in. My father hears most of the track rumors. If this weren't my first project since returning to Tanner, it might be different. I haven't proven myself yet."

"Of course I understand." He stepped closer. "I don't want to make things hard for you. I'll do my best to keep things on a more professional footing."

The warmth of his body drew her, his scent washed over her. Her voice was husky when she said, "I might… believe you, if you didn't move closer when you said it."

His smile was knowing. "You're so sure it was me who moved?"

She lost herself in the moment, so glad to be here with him. "No, I'm not sure at all. That's what scares me."

"You and I," his breath was warm on her cheek, "have work to do. We'll continue this later." His voice was layered with meaning.

Goose bumps rose on her arms.

"I think it's time for *me* to take a walk," he said.

Nodding, she refused to watch him leave because she knew he'd be grinning. Instead, Jamie picked up where she'd left off with the motor.

A few minutes later, he set a water bottle on the table for her. "Gotta stay hydrated." Then he went over to the practice motor to tinker with the poor, damaged piece of equipment.

Time stopped as she lost herself in her work. Then her wrench slipped and she scraped her knuckles. Swearing under her breath, she wiped the sweat from her eyes.

Ryan walked over and took the wrench from her and placed it on the table.

When she started to protest, he pressed his finger against her lips. "No arguing. It's nearly four and if you don't get some sleep you're going to really hurt yourself. That's not going to help anyone."

Her eyes were gritty, her vision blurred. "I guess you're right."

"Why don't you use the cot in the office?"

She glanced at the cot in the corner. "I'll be more comfortable here, near the car."

And near him. Jamie was too tired to censor the thought.

Kicking off her shoes, she settled herself on the cot, pulling the lightweight cotton blanket beneath her chin. She turned to the wall and closed her eyes, inhaling Ryan's scent on the pillow.

Exhaustion stilled thoughts that otherwise would have raced through her mind. She snuggled deeper into the cot and drifted off to sleep.

RYAN HAD COFFEE brewing in the office when Bill arrived the next morning before seven.

"Hey, where's Jamie?" His question was casual, too casual.

"Asleep on the cot since four."

"Good. I was afraid she'd try and work straight through. I've seen a lot of good mechanics screw up that way."

"Yeah, me, too. Will you do me a favor? Go get some breakfast sandwiches?"

"Sure. You buy, I'll fly."

"Thanks." Ryan withdrew his wallet and handed him the cash.

When Bill returned, Ryan went to wake Jamie.

She was sitting up on the cot, rubbing her still sleepy eyes. "Why didn't you wake me? What time is it?" There was a hint of panic in her voice.

"A little after seven."

She groaned. "I didn't mean to sleep this late."

"I don't consider three hours shirking your duties.

It's just realistic to get some rest. Besides, Bill brought breakfast. After you eat, you'll feel good as new and we'll tackle that motor."

"What about you?"

"I figure I'll go to the hauler once the rest of the guys arrive."

Jamie watched Ryan over the rim of her coffee cup. His face was scruffy, his hair mussed and he looked anything but a glamorous driver.

And she fell just a little more in love with him.

It was nice to have someone care whether she ate and slept, whether she might hurt herself due to fatigue. And she had to admit to feeling much more alert after a few hours sleep and a good breakfast. The coffee didn't hurt either.

The rest of the guys straggled in as she went over to her work table. They were helping load the hauler today. The car would be the last item loaded, when she finished the motor, that is. If nothing else went wrong, she just might be able to do it.

Fortunately, Ryan seemed to understand what she was up against. He touched her shoulder. "If you need anything, just let me know. I'll be over at the hauler going over stats."

"I will."

"I'd be glad to help, but I get the feeling you'd rather work alone."

She smiled, nodded, then tuned him out.

RYAN EYED the clock. It was eight p.m. He'd tried to keep from dogging Jamie's tracks, but the compulsion was almost overwhelming. As if by watching her every move, he could control the outcome.

Fortunately, she didn't seem to notice. Intensity radiated from her in waves, her movements quick and sure. She was in her zone, something that would have been poetic to watch, if his career didn't hinge on her ability to build an engine faster than most. Maybe even faster than her father.

She'd removed her Pistons cap and replaced it with a bandana tied like a headband. From the way she swiped her arm across her forehead, he surmised even that didn't absorb enough perspiration.

"If you're going to just stand there, you could get me two water bottles." The edge in her voice made him smile. She was sweaty, cranky and darn near irresistible. He'd never met a woman like her.

And might not ever again.

The thought made him oddly uncomfortable. As if there was something he should do about it.

Because he already felt she was his. The hairs on the back of his neck prickled at the thought. He didn't want her depending on him, did he?

Ryan went to the small refrigerator and selected two ice cold water bottles. He set them on the table near where she worked.

Jamie stopped. She twisted the cap off a bottle and took a swig out of it. Then she poured the rest over her head and down her T-shirt. "Evaporative cooling."

"Effective." And darn near unnerving for the guy watching her. The T-shirt clung to her chest, emphasizing her curves.

Rolling her shoulders, she worked the kinks out.

He moved behind her, kneading her shoulders with his hands.

"Oh, that's wonderful," she groaned.

"Can't have my engine technician seizing up on me."

Yeah, right. He simply had to have his hands on her in some way, though not the way he longed for. His desire to ease her discomfort was nearly as strong as his desire to make love to her. And that was scary.

"Are you okay? Need a break?" he asked.

"I can handle it. We're almost there."

"How much longer?"

"Two hours. Maybe a little longer."

"Then we can get the hauler on the road by midnight."

"As my daddy would say, 'God willing and the creek don't rise.' I'd better get to it. Thanks for the water and the shoulder massage. You really know how to treat your people."

"I try." Ryan's ears grew warm. He had no doubt they were probably pink, a dead giveaway. Fact was, he'd never given one of his team a shoulder massage and would rather walk barefoot over hot coals.

JAMIE WAS BARELY aware of Ryan as she moved to the engine. A good thing she was able to tune out distractions, because he was *very* distracting. Not only was he adept at working out the knots in her shoulders, but he also seemed to understand what she needed before she did. She couldn't help but wonder what other needs he might anticipate.

Redirecting her thoughts, Jamie forced herself to focus. Soon she was back in the groove, creating the best damn Tanner motor ever.

Almost exactly two hours later, she stepped back from the work table and simply stared at her creation. Steel and chrome gleamed under the fluorescent lighting.

Jamie wanted to exclaim, "Ta-da." Too childish. Taking a bow to an invisible crowd seemed too egotistical. But the applause coming from her cheering section of one seemed just right.

She turned and walked into Ryan's open arms. And felt as if she'd come home.

"I'm proud of you," he murmured against her hair.

"I'm proud of me, too." She raised her eyes, meeting his gaze.

He kissed her, tender, reverent, apparently not caring that she was grease-smudged and damp with perspiration.

Jamie was nearly giddy with her accomplishment, relieved that she'd managed the nearly impossible.

Ryan's arms tightened around her and rational thought fled. She wrapped her arms around his waist, ignoring the whispers in her head cautioning her to take it slow. This was right. *They* were right.

She murmured his name and deepened the kiss, sinking in to him. Cool air caressed her flesh as he slid his hands under her shirt and trailed his palms along her lower back.

She moved against him, trying to get closer.

He gripped her hips and pulled her tight against him.

Jamie thought she'd come unglued at the intensity of her response. Her breathing grew shallow, her senses swam, losing herself in Ryan.

He trailed kisses down her neck, caressing the hollow

at her throat with his tongue. His breath was warm on her neck as he nibbled on her earlobe. His whiskers rasped the sensitive skin along her jaw right before he found her mouth again.

"Jamie." He murmured against her lips, cupping her rear end with his hands.

Heat seared her nerve endings. She wanted to make love with this man who accepted her for who she was.

Then he stopped kissing, stopped caressing. Simply rested his forehead against hers.

She twined her arms around his neck to prevent him from moving away.

Gently grasping her chin with his hand, he said, "I want you more than I've wanted any other woman. But we're not kids—we need to think about what we're doing. I don't want to destroy your chance of being the person you were meant to be…I care about you too much for that."

Regret replaced the passion in his eyes.

Jamie swallowed her disappointment. She gathered the courage to say what was in her heart. "I think I'm falling for you, Ryan."

She closed her eyes tight, afraid she might see pity in his eyes. Afraid she sounded like another besotted track groupie.

"Hey." His voice was warm. "Open those beautiful green eyes. I *know* I'm falling for you. And it scares the hell out of me."

"So where do we go from here?"

"First, we have a race to win." His grin was crooked. "And I'd like to have you by my side at Darlington. Because it will mean a lot to know you're cheering me on. And because you're the best damn engine technician I've ever seen."

"There's nowhere else I'd rather be." She stood on tiptoe and kissed him lingeringly.

"Let's go tell the guys they can install the engine, run the dyno and load up."

Jamie nodded, smiling. She ignored the fact that they hadn't discussed a future. That would come later. She hoped.

CHAPTER SIXTEEN

JAMIE OPERATED the hoist while Bill guided the motor into the engine compartment. They all worked together to get it connected and ready for start up.

"You want to do the honors?" Bill asked her.

"I'm too nervous. How about Ryan?"

"Ryan? Start her up?"

Ryan's eyes met hers. A smile twitched at his lips and she knew he'd caught the double meaning. "Sure. I'd love to."

Jamie's cheeks grew warm. She hoped nobody could tell she was blushing.

Ryan slid in through the window.

Jamie held her breath. What was he waiting for?

His grin was wicked. He had to know the suspense was killing her.

Finally, he started the motor. It turned over immediately and roared to life. The reverberation shot through the soles of her feet, making her pulse pound, her breath quicken. Her baby sounded beautiful. Absolutely beautiful.

Ryan wished he could carry this image of Jamie forever. Her smile lit the room and warmed his heart. He shook his head. Man, he had it bad.

Somehow he'd managed to keep his hands off her as the crew readied the car to go on the hauler. Hydraulics lifted the platform so the car could be placed near the roof.

He sighed with relief when the whole operation was complete. Leaning down, he spoke close to Jamie's ear. "I'd love to take you to Darlington by private jet, but we fly commercial. Want me to try to get you on my flight tomorrow morning?"

She glanced up at him, smiling. "I'd like that."

"Better get back to your hotel and catch a few hours sleep."

He thought he detected a hint of disappointment in her eyes. He hoped so. Because he would have liked nothing better than to take her back to his condo and make love to her all night long.

"I might just sleep on the cot in the shop."

"No way. It'd drive me crazy knowing you were nearby."

She raised an eyebrow, a skeptical glint in her eye.

His voice was low when he said, "I'd invite you back to my place, but it's not a good idea. How about we take things slow over the next few days and decide where we want this to go after Darlington?"

"You're probably right."

He glanced around and kissed her quickly. "I'll walk you to your car."

"Uh-uh. Remember what happened in the parking lot at Talladega?"

"Boy, do I." His body went into heightened alert just thinking about it. "I'll walk you to the gate."

"Okay." She picked up her tool duffel and headed

toward the parking lot. A few steps away, she glanced over her shoulder. "You coming?"

He shook himself out of his trance. "Sure. Just admiring the view." And what a view it was. He jogged to catch up, suspecting that he'd follow this woman anywhere.

The thought was scary as hell, but fascinating at the same time. But when she slid her small, callused hand in his, he felt his heart doing donuts in his chest.

JAMIE AWOKE Thursday morning amazingly refreshed after only six hours of sleep. Yet, she was strangely indecisive.

Her T-shirt wardrobe now seemed woefully inadequate for flying with Ryan. She longed for something more feminine, something to make his eyes light up.

Shaking her head, Jamie reminded herself that Ryan's eyes lit with appreciation even when she was dressed in grubby work clothes. Hallelujah, a man who loved her just the way she was!

Love? He hadn't come close to uttering the *L word.* A good thing, she told herself, because bringing love into it would make their relationship so much more complex. But darn it, she wanted his love anyway.

Jamie groaned. Her world had shifted, everything she thought was true simply didn't apply anymore. She was falling in love with Ryan Pearce and there didn't seem to be a thing she could do about it. Worse yet, she wasn't sure she wanted to.

She glanced at her watch. Better get moving. Throwing on one of her old faithful shirts and a pair of jeans, she headed for the door.

Fortunately, traffic was light and she arrived at Ryan's condominium on time. He was waiting out front, carry-on in hand.

He'd opened the passenger door and slid in the seat almost before she came to a stop. "Hi."

His smile warmed her.

"Hi, yourself."

He settled in and buckled his seat belt. Through quick glances, she was able to drink in small details. His hair was damp, as if he'd just gotten out of the shower. She was almost disappointed to see that he'd shaved last night's sexy stubble.

Jamie touched the sensitive pink spot near her mouth. A gentle reminder of how intoxicating his kisses could be.

Focus, Jamie.

"Is the hauler in Darlington yet?" she asked.

"Got there a couple hours ago."

"Did the car ride okay?"

"It always does. They always double and triple check."

"Good. I'm glad you were able to get me on your flight." This was worse than morning-after-sex conversation. Why were they suddenly so awkward?

"Yeah, me, too. Thanks for the lift."

"No problem. I have to return the rental to the airport anyway."

They chatted about inconsequential stuff the rest of the way to the airport. By the time they boarded, some of the awkwardness had abated.

Jamie might have enjoyed the flight if they had been a regular couple. Or not a couple at all, even in the most tenuous sense—which they were.

She leaned back in her seat, imagining vacationing

with Ryan. Traveling someplace exotic; maybe watching the Le Mans in Europe.

As it was, nervous excitement stirred in her stomach. The man she loved was racing her engine this weekend. It was a once in a lifetime opportunity seeing the motor she'd built for Tanner run with the best.

But behind the excitement, uneasiness lurked. The motor had sounded good, tested well, but they hadn't seen it run on a track. Or even in a residential neighborhood, for that matter. There could be all sorts of surprises waiting for her in Darlington.

One complication she hadn't anticipated was the urgent message waiting for her when she landed. While Ryan made arrangements for the rental car, she called Tom.

"Hey Tom, what's wrong?"

"Where the hell have you been? I've been trying to reach you since yesterday."

She didn't like his tone. "I was busting my butt for our respective employer, building a new engine for the Pearce Racing Team."

"And why didn't you bother to share that information with me? Why'd I have to hear it from Dad?"

Jamie suppressed a groan. No wonder he was ticked off. "I'm sorry, Tom. Things happened so fast, I forgot to keep you in the loop. In case you didn't know, building a motor from scratch in three days is darn near miraculous. Then throw in parts delays and a burglary at the Pearce garage. I've been running on pure adrenaline."

"A break-in? I hope they didn't get anything crucial."

"A few parts, but mostly just made a huge mess."

"I don't like the sound of that. Don't take any chances, okay?"

"I won't." Her voice was husky. For once, Tom's concern seemed genuine instead of overbearing. Or had her perception simply shifted?

"Have you committed to paying for the motor?" he asked.

"Only if it turns out it was our fault. The carburetor from the initial engine was stolen in the break-in. It's going to be difficult to prove one way or the other."

"Good. Then we don't pay."

This was the penny-pinching brother she knew. "Tom, that's not the way Tanner does business."

He sighed. "I know. But a free motor would really cut our profit margin for the quarter."

"I still have the O-rings from the carburetor. They might give us some insight."

"Let's hope so. Don't make any commitments on paying for that motor until you talk to me. Remember, I want to be kept in the loop."

"My credibility is going to be shot if I have to run to you for permission to do my job. Believe me, I'm not going to promise the moon. Especially if it turns out we're not at fault."

"I guess I'll have to trust your judgment." He hesitated. "I'm thinking about flying out to Darlington for the race. We can discuss it more then."

Jamie replied in frustration, "Do you have any idea what kind of authority I had in the engineering department? This is small change by comparison."

"I'm sure it is. But it's our family's small change—

that makes all the difference. Let's not debate it over the phone. I'll look you up when I get to the track."

Jamie gave in to the inevitable, but not before toying with him a bit. "I'm glad you're coming. That way if the engine blows, you can field the press questions."

"But, but—"

"Only joking, Tom. It's not going to blow. You are way too easy to tease."

"You have the unfair advantage of knowing which buttons to push."

"It works both ways. I better get going."

"Wait. Jamie?"

"Yes?"

"Good luck."

"I don't need luck. I have skill." She hoped her bluster fooled him. He didn't need to know her stomach was doing cartwheels because of the importance of this race—to her, to her family and maybe most importantly, to Ryan.

She said her goodbyes and shut her phone as Ryan approached.

"Bad news?" he asked.

"No, just my baby brother checking on me. He can be a real pain in the rear sometimes, but we seem to be working it out."

"That's good. I think I'd be willing to risk the rivalry stuff for a brother or sister."

She rolled her eyes. "Spoken like a true only child."

The fleeting sadness in his eyes made her want to erase her thoughtless remark. From what he'd said, his mom had always been working. No siblings, no father. He'd probably been a very lonely little boy.

"You had friends, didn't you?"

"A few. But I couldn't do a lot of the stuff they did. We didn't have extra cash for movies and birthday parties."

"So what did you do?"

"Read anything I could get my hands on about racing. Watched the few races that were on TV."

Her heart ached at the bleak picture he painted. She touched his arm. "And dreamed of being a driver?"

"Not being *a* driver. Being *the* driver. That meant the Winston Cup in those days." He glanced at his watch. "Come on, I've rented a car."

She let him evade the subject. But she longed to know all about him, what had made him into the man he was today.

And when they found their rental car in the lot, Jamie fell just a little further in love with him. "A Mustang."

His grin was sheepish, the tips of his ears turned pink. "I noticed you like them."

She threw her arms around his neck and kissed him. "Thank you! No one's ever bothered to notice before."

Tracing her cheek with his finger, he murmured, "Oh, I did."

Jamie swallowed hard. God help her, she didn't know if she was strong enough to walk away from this man. Hopefully, it wouldn't be necessary.

They went straight to the hauler when they arrived at the track. It felt warm and familiar, a cocoon that represented everything wonderful about Ryan.

"Hey, Ryan," the guys called as they joined them under the awning. "Hey, Jamie."

A few couldn't seem to look her in the eye. They knew about her relationship with Ryan.

Bill came over to confer with Ryan. "I've got you set up for practice this afternoon. I'll see if I can get you another short session tomorrow before qualifying."

"Sounds good. With a brand new motor, we can expect some kinks to work out. Even one built by a master technician."

He didn't have to say it, but she appreciated the sentiment all the same. "Adjustments go with the territory no matter who builds the motor."

She glanced at her watch. "I need to check in at a hotel. You mind if I stay where the crew stays? If they aren't fully booked."

"Not at all. Makes sense, since it's the closest, reasonably priced hotel. I'm sure there'll be a cancellation and they'll give you a room."

"I'll give you the address and a map," Bill said.

"Great."

"Here're the keys to the rental car." Ryan tossed them to her. "You're coming back this afternoon, aren't you?"

"Of course. I'll be here in time to see your first practice run. You mind if I leave my tools here?"

"Go ahead."

Bill handed Ryan a sheaf of papers. "Here're the specs we're running. See if you want any changes before practice."

"I'll see you later." Jamie put her bag in the cabinet and left Ryan in Bill's very capable care.

It was odd walking through the parking lot alone. She and Ryan had been almost inseparable for the past couple of days and she felt his absence acutely. The drive wasn't nearly as entertaining without him. And the hotel room felt empty once she checked in. Or maybe she felt empty.

Jamie stowed her carry-on by the bed and sat down. But restlessness soon had her up and moving. Would it look odd if she hurried back to the track? As if she simply couldn't live without Ryan?

No, not to anyone but her guilty conscience.

Decision made, Jamie grabbed her purse and headed out the door. One thing was sure, it was going to be a very intense weekend if she had to vet every action, every sentence. No wonder people avoided workplace relationships like the plague.

RYAN STOOD next to the Number 63 car, resting his forearm against the roof. He tried not to anticipate how the car would run. Or think about jinxes and bad luck. He firmly believed a man made his own luck in life. It was just a matter of how a guy handled all the crap thrown at him.

"Whew, glad I made it in time. I got delayed in traffic."

He turned at the sound of Jamie's voice. Now he knew it would be a good run. Because nothing bad could happen with Jamie smiling at him that way. And if it did, they'd work through it together. Just as they'd worked together building the new motor.

"I'm about ready to start her up. I'm glad you're here," he said.

She adjusted her Tanner Motors cap. "I'm kind of nervous."

He wanted to wrap his arms around her and tell her everything would be okay. But even during practice, the stands teemed with fans and media alike. He opted for verbal reassurance instead. "It's going to be fine."

She held his gaze. "Yes, I think you're right."

Bill jogged up. "It's time."

Ryan nodded and donned his helmet, adjusting the strap.

"Good luck," Jamie murmured.

He grinned. "Thanks."

The practice laps went like a dream. The car handled well. It was one of those Zen experiences when everything came together perfectly. When he pulled into the pits, he saw Bill and Jamie exchange a high five. The rest of the crew followed suit.

He levered himself out of the car and let out a whoop. Their luck had turned.

When he reached Jamie, he lifted her off the ground and swung her around. Her smile warmed him, making his chest constrict with how right it seemed. Ryan, Jamie, racing together as a team.

He set her back on the ground.

Bill flashed him a look. "Easy does it, son. The press is here."

Ryan swallowed hard, surveying the stands. "Damn, I forgot."

Bill clapped him on the back, nudging him in the direction of the hauler. "No harm done. But best be careful. You wouldn't want to hurt Jamie's reputation."

Jamie's face paled. "I wasn't thinking, either." She fell into step beside them. "It was as much my fault as Ryan's. Besides, it was harmless."

Bill adjusted his cap. "The motor sounded good. How about the handling?"

"Perfect. Don't change a thing." Ryan felt more positive than he had in a long time.

"Still want that extra practice run tomorrow?"

"Couldn't hurt."

"Looks like you're done today then. Tomorrow will be a full day."

Ryan nodded. Between practice, a sponsor's event and qualifying, Friday would be busy.

Bill angled his head in Jamie's direction. "I mean, if you'd like to go somewhere besides the track, now would be the time. Like dinner out."

"Oh, yeah. Jamie, you want to grab a bite?"

Bill smiled, as if his star pupil had just caught on.

Jamie impulsively kissed Bill on the cheek. "You're an old softie, you know."

His face reddened. "Yeah, but don't let it get around. Those guys'll walk all over me."

"Your secret's safe with me."

She turned to Ryan. "I'd love to. Am I dressed okay?"

"You look beautiful."

Even in her faded jeans and T-shirt, she felt beautiful.

They ate at a rustic place that elevated prime rib to an art form. She'd removed her cap, fluffed her hair and was dressed just fine for the laid-back atmosphere.

They ate and talked and laughed, just like on a real date. With a jolt, Jamie realized it was a real date. And when they returned to the track several hours later, she was eager for a good night kiss. With the promise of more.

She was disappointed when they pulled into the

parking lot and Ryan said, “You can drop me off at the gate.”

“Sure.” She tried for a nonchalant tone, but apparently failed.

He cupped her chin. His voice was warm and low. “I’d invite you back to the motor home, but I don’t trust myself not to seduce you.”

That was a bad thing?

“I guess I’m glad one of us is thinking ahead. Because there’s a part of me that would love to go home with you and see what happens. But you were right when you suggested we take it slow this weekend.”

“I need to focus on the race. Qualifying tomorrow is important. And I need to have my head straight Saturday night.”

Jamie tried to make sense of his words. “I wouldn’t interfere with your racing.”

“Just realize I might not be able to pay much attention to you.”

Understanding dawned. “I wouldn’t think of distracting you any more than you would have tried to distract me while I built that motor.”

He smiled. “I guess not. This is new territory for me. Be patient till I can get it right.”

“I’m not usually very patient, but when the reward is worthwhile, I can wait.”

“Good.” He leaned forward and kissed her. “I have the feeling it will be *very* worthwhile.”

She cupped his face with her hands, drawing him close.

He made a noise deep in his throat, part moan, part growl. Deepening the kiss, Jamie’s world receded until the only thing that mattered was Ryan.

It could have been minutes—or hours—later when Ryan drew away. "I'd better go before all my good intentions are out the window."

"Mine, too."

She watched him get out of the car and close the door. At the gate he turned and waved.

Jamie touched her lips as he walked away, leaving her world empty again.

CHAPTER SEVENTEEN

BY NOON on Friday, Jamie was restless. Fortunately, Ryan practiced at twelve-thirty and it was pure joy to watch him coax peak performance from the car.

Jamie was proud of the job she'd done. And after the race, everyone—even her mother—would acknowledge she was the logical person to fill her father's shoes.

But her pleasure at a job well done was soon overshadowed by the tedium of having absolutely nothing to do. By two o'clock she was bored stiff. Literally. Her muscles protested the enforced inactivity after pushing herself physically for nearly four days.

Walking relieved the soreness a bit and gave her the excuse to wander in search of Ryan. She found him holding court on the infield with Divine Products' bigwigs and their nearest and dearest five-hundred friends.

Jamie was tempted to join him if only because she wasn't accustomed to feeling like a useless appendage. If they'd been back at Charlotte, she would have gone to the shop and worked on the practice motor.

Flipping open her cell, she called Tom. He wanted her to keep him in the loop, didn't he?

When it went into his voice mail, she hit disconnect.

Tapping her fingers, she contemplated calling her parents. But why chance having her mother rain on her parade?

She wandered inside the hauler and watched the activity. One of the technicians worked on suspension parts at a workbench.

Jamie longed to grab her tools and join him. But even a crew as small as Ryan's had very specific functions. The technician probably knew more about suspension than she could ever hope to learn. Or wanted to, for that matter. But few knew engines like she did. It was a yin-yang kind of thing.

She wondered how the wives and girlfriends stood being on the road. How did they manage to carve out lives for themselves when they flew to the track every weekend for the duration of the season?

Jamie took a doughnut from the box on the kitchen counter and placed it on a napkin, licking the sweet goo from her fingers.

Then she stopped short. She was contemplating the life of a track significant other. And about to gorge herself on sweets. That could mean only one thing—she wanted Ryan in a permanent, till-death-do-us-part kind of way.

"You're frowning and sighing again," Ryan teased.

She turned and flew into his arms.

"Hey, what's this about?"

"I missed you. And I'm bored." Jamie winced at the petulance in her own voice. And here she'd thought Sheila had been self-centered.

"I missed you, too. It's nice not to be talking about incontinence."

She chuckled. "It could be worse."

"Yeah? How?" Then he held up his hand. "No, I don't want to know. I'm very pleased with my sponsorship and proud to drive the Divine Products car."

"You rehearse that a lot?"

"Don't have to. I have it memorized. I say it just about every week. But I mean it every time. They are really good to me."

"I bet."

"The sponsors were very happy with what they saw in practice, by the way. And I owe a lot of that to you. You built one mean engine."

"I aim to please."

"And you do." He glanced over his shoulder to where the technician had his back turned and hauled her close. "You're amazing."

A lump formed in her throat at the admiration in his eyes. Along with a touch of lust and something she dared not name. Something deeper than just affection.

"You're not so bad yourself."

He dipped his head to kiss her.

She met him halfway, making an almost imperceptible whimper. She wanted to be with him like this forever.

The sound of clapping cut through her haze of need.

Ryan released her and turned.

Jamie's heart sank. She was busted, big time. But she wouldn't go down without a fight.

Standing tall, she demanded, "What're you staring at, Tom?"

Crossing his arms, his expression was downright forbidding. "I'm watching a very promising career go down the tubes, that's what."

"This is none of your business."

Her brother approached them. "Your shirt says differently. 'Tanner Performance Motors.' You're representing not only the family, but the business."

"It's not her fault." Ryan stepped between them.

"No, nothing ever is."

Ryan's fists clenched. "What's that supposed to mean?"

Tom replied, "Jamie has a long history of being able to do no wrong."

Jamie grasped Ryan's arm as he swore under his breath. "No, Ryan. Tom's right."

Refusing to be baited, she looked levelly at her brother. "I'm sorry, Tom. I'll be more careful about my actions when I'm wearing the Tanner uniform. It won't happen again."

His shoulders relaxed. "Maybe I overreacted. Please be more careful next time." He glanced at Ryan. "And Pearce, you better treat my sister right. She's no pit lizard."

"I care a lot about Jamie. *I'm* not the one treating her with disrespect."

"Point taken. Keep it that way."

Jamie smothered a smile. "I know you're just looking out for me. It's…kind of nice."

Tom glanced away. "Yeah, well that's what brothers do. The rumors are already flying about you and Pearce. That's one of the reasons I came down for the qualifying."

Jamie swallowed hard. "Rumors?"

He raised an eyebrow. "You know there's a grapevine that would rival the CIA. If Dad had his doctor's clearance to fly, he'd here right now. Mom, too. As it is, you'll have a lot of explaining to do when you get home."

TOM TANNER SAT in the stands and waited for qualifying to begin. The buzz was that Pearce was good, but his equipment wasn't top-drawer. Tom wanted to see him kick butt with a Tanner engine.

He just wasn't as sure he wanted the guy messing with his sister. For the first time, he felt protective toward Jamie—a reversal of their roles growing up.

Tom raised his binoculars. The drivers started their engines. It was something that never ceased to make his pulse jump. What he wouldn't give to be down there listening closely to the motor Jamie had built. Then he would know if she'd come through for them.

But he'd decided to sit in the stands—less family drama that way. Tom kicked back to watch each car. The qualifying was fast and furious, with Pearce getting second.

Tom's spirits rose. Pearce might give them the opportunity to take Tanner Motors to a whole new level. If he didn't mess things up with Jamie that is.

AFTER QUALIFYING, Ryan was more careful about how he approached Jamie coming off the field. He grinned and winked, but didn't get closer than ten feet.

She smiled and nodded, giving him the thumbs up. Good. She understood he was simply trying to make things easier for her.

Bill clapped him on the back. "Looks like the car's still set up right. Any adjustments needed?"

"It was pushing a tiny bit in Turn Three. Other than that, it's darn near perfect."

"We'll tweak the suspension."

Ryan thanked his team and accepted their congratulations. It was a team effort—no one was a star, including him.

They walked toward the hauler, Bill jawing about what he'd heard other teams were doing to get a few extra rpm. Ryan was aware of Jamie blending in with the rest of the crew.

Once inside, he allowed himself to go near her. They exchanged a long, smoldering gaze, then discussed the way the car had performed.

Ryan could visualize this scenario race after race, track after track. He swallowed hard. He'd allowed himself to get more involved with Jamie than he'd intended. What had happened to his plans to avoid relationships while he was racing?

"Now *you're* frowning and sighing," Jamie teased. Her eyes were pretty when they sparkled with mischief.

"I don't sigh."

"After that nice qualifying, I'd think you'd be dancing."

"It *is* pretty sweet."

"Then why the frown a moment ago?"

"Nothing."

"It was something, but I won't press. If it involved me, you'd talk to me, wouldn't you?"

"Sure." What a crock. It most certainly involved her and he had no intention of talking about it till he had it worked out in his mind.

"Have you got plans for an early supper? I thought

I'd take you to an Italian place I heard about. I'm buying."

He grinned. "Hey, if you're buying, count me in."

"Good." She hesitated. "About that stuff my brother said. I appreciate you cooling things down in public. I haven't been very good at taking things slow, like we agreed."

He touched her arm. "Neither have I. But we'll start over. No liplocks unless we're alone, I promise."

A forlorn expression passed over her face.

"What's wrong?"

"Nothing. Except we're hardly ever alone."

Her statement hit him between the eyes. His life during the season was scheduled to the hilt—he'd simply never paid much attention until now. He infused his voice with false optimism. "We'll just have to make some opportunities."

He turned over the problem in his mind while Jamie went to get a soda. The only good solution made him break out in a sweat.

If they were married, they wouldn't have to sneak around. Nobody could disparage Jamie for random PDAs with her husband. And they would have time alone at the end of the day, sharing the cozy bed in his motor home or holed up in his condo in Charlotte. He could even imagine some fairly creative ways they could be alone in his shop.

Shaking his head, Ryan felt like things with Jamie were moving too fast, his feelings for her too intense. His only choice seemed to be hanging on for the ride. For a guy who had done everything according to plan in working his way up the NASCAR ranks, the thought of suddenly letting go petrified him.

CHAPTER EIGHTEEN

JAMIE TOLD herself she hadn't chosen the restaurant because it was out of town, away from the track. All the same, she surreptitiously glanced around when they arrived.

She exhaled slowly when she didn't see anyone she recognized from the track. Then someone stopped Ryan for an autograph and she realized they were never totally out of the public eye. Except maybe in his shop in Charlotte or in the hauler. That might narrow their world considerably.

But she soon forgot her worries. Seated in a booth with tall backs, they were secluded in their own little world.

"How's your dad doing?" Ryan asked.

Jamie groaned. "I meant to call him earlier and I forgot."

"Go ahead and call him now. Just tell me what you want to eat and I'll order for you."

She did, then dialed her parents' number. Her mother answered.

"I'm so sorry I missed Daddy's birthday. How's he doing?"

"About the same. Is there something going on there,

Honey? Tom mentioned something about flying out to check the engine you built for the Pearce team. But I get the feeling his reason was more to check on you."

"Everything's fine, Mom. I talked to Tom, you have nothing to worry about."

"Then you're not involved with that driver?"

Jamie closed her eyes. There was a conversation she didn't want to have. At best, she could stall. "We'll talk when I get home. May I talk to Daddy? I don't have long."

The waitress came by and Ryan gave her the drink order while her father picked up the phone.

"Hi, Daddy."

"Hi, Kitten, it's good to hear your voice."

"I wanted to wish you a belated happy birthday. How're you doing?"

"Bored. Don't know how people stand all this daytime television. I'm going to talk to that doctor about returning to work early. Otherwise, I'll go stir crazy."

Now Jamie knew why she couldn't sit still; it was genetic. "Daddy, it's important you heal from your surgery. You've been through a trauma."

"Not as much as when I heard some of the goings-ons at Darlington."

Wincing, Jamie said, "You don't have to worry about me. I'm one-hundred percent dedicated to Tanner."

He snorted. "Jamie Lynn, you always were a terrible liar. Be careful. And make me proud."

Her eyes misted. She cleared her throat. "Always, Daddy, always."

They chatted for another minute, then Jamie told him she had to go.

Ryan grasped her hand across the table. "You okay?"

She nodded.

"I can tell you're upset."

"Tom's telling the truth. Daddy's heard rumors about us. He doesn't sound happy, then he told me to make him proud." She shredded the paper straw cover. "That's all I've ever wanted, Ryan. To make him proud."

"You do and you will."

"I hope so," she murmured.

TOM CLIMBED the stairs on the Pearce hauler.

"Tom." Ryan Pearce came over and shook his hand. "Good to see you."

"Thanks for the invite. I have to admit I was a bit surprised when I received your call."

"Family is important to Jamie."

And whatever was important to Jamie was apparently important to Pearce. The guy rose a couple notches in Tom's estimation. And eased his mind a bit.

Jamie approached. "Tom, what a surprise."

"Ryan invited me to watch the Busch race."

Patting his arm, she said, "As long as you behave. There are sodas in the ice chest."

"Plenty of food inside, too." Ryan said.

"Thanks."

He helped himself to a soda and glanced around, nodding to a few familiar faces. Nobody he knew by name.

It wasn't hard to locate Jamie's bright blond hair where she stood at the rail next to Ryan. They stood close, but not in an overtly sexual way.

Both smiled and laughed a lot. The intensity of their connection nearly vibrated in the air.

Tom sucked in a breath. Jamie was in love. And it appeared Ryan returned her feelings.

The idea should have made him happy. If Jamie went on the road with the Pearce team, she'd leave the field wide open at Tanner. No more worrying about her usurping his position.

But mostly it made him sad. Because she had apparently found something that had evaded him for twenty-eight years.

AS THE RACE was coming to an end Ryan checked his cell phone display and sighed. "I better take this."

Jamie rose. "I'll go make sure Tom's behaving himself."

Ryan nodded, flipping open his phone. "Hi, Mom."

"Ryan, how are you?"

"Good. What's going on?"

"I just wanted to talk to you before the race tomorrow. Well, you know…in case something happens."

"I'll be fine, Mom. Nothing's going to happen."

"It's a mother's job to worry." Then she went into her usual litany of fears.

And he went through his usual litany of facts to set her mind at ease. Same old, same old. He wondered if baseball players fielded tense phone calls from their mothers before every game.

It sure wasn't a confidence booster. He always made an effort to keep his thoughts positive, so her fears didn't become a self-fulfilling prophecy.

The conversation soon lagged.

"I've met someone, Mom." The words slipped out before he could stop himself.

"Is it…serious?"

"I think so. Her name is Jamie. She's special."

"Oh." Her voice lowered. "I hope you know what you're doing."

"I think so," he lied.

"Oh, Ryan, after all we've been through, you should know better. Racing isn't the life for a married man. Especially for a man like you."

"You mean a man like Dad?"

"It's in your genes, Ryan."

"What is?" For once, he wanted her to spell it out. Maybe she'd realize how twisted it sounded.

She hesitated. "Carousing."

"If you mean cheating, I don't intend to follow in Dad's footsteps. I really care about Jamie."

"I'm sure you do. But sometimes that's not enough."

He shouldn't even try to talk to her about something so personal. It never ended well. "I need to go, Mom. Was there anything else?"

"No. I just wanted to hear your voice. And wish you luck."

"Thanks. I'll talk to you later."

"Goodbye, dear."

He closed the phone as Jamie approached.

"Something wrong?" she asked.

"Just my mom and her usual pre-race pep talk."

"Do I detect a note of sarcasm?"

"Yeah, I tend to get defensive." He shrugged. "How's Tom doing?"

"Fine. Rehashing the race with some of the guys." She sat next to him and grasped his hand. "It was nice of you to invite him."

"On the whole, he seems like a decent guy. I can't fault him for being concerned about you."

"I suppose not." She hesitated. "Does your mom live in Charlotte?"

"Nope. Atlanta. She comes to visit a couple times a year. And I try to see her when I race in her neck of the woods."

"You said she worked a couple jobs when you were growing up. What did she do?"

"She waitressed because the tips were good."

"Does she still work?"

"Yeah, but I intend to make sure that's not necessary. Once I'm solid in the Chase, I can start sending more home."

"More? I don't know many guys who'd do that. Most of them are still mooching off their folks."

"She's my mom. I couldn't live with myself if I didn't help out. That's why…sometimes I wonder if I should have stayed with a steady, reliable income as a mechanic."

"You would quit racing for your mother?"

He hesitated, unable to confide one of his strongest fears. "I don't know. Only hope to hell I never have to make that choice."

Because if he couldn't let go of his dream, even for his mother, that would make him as low as his dad. But he didn't intend to dwell on the thought.

Ryan grasped her hand. "Enough about me. I want to know more about you. Tell me about the Poultry Princess stuff."

She did and he was fascinated. "It takes courage for you to stand up to your mom. You've got the guts to follow your dreams and make them happen."

"You give me more credit than I deserve. I ran away to Michigan for twelve years, hiding from what I really wanted because I was too scared to fight for it."

"It's hard to stand up for what you believe when you know everyone else wants you to be something different."

Jamie nodded. "When I was little, I resented every second I had to spend pretending I enjoyed playing with dolls. All I could focus on was getting time with a wrench in my hand."

His chest ached at the sadness in her eyes. "You shouldn't have been pressured to be something you weren't."

"I won't ever do that to my children. I'll make sure they know how special they are without having to fit someone else's mould."

"You'll be a great mom someday." The thought came out of nowhere.

"I'm thirty-five years old. My somedays are numbered."

"I wondered if you'd decided not to have kids." Had he *hoped* she'd decided not to have children? Maybe because he might risk having a life with both racing and a wife, but not the children part?

He held his breath while she mulled his question.

When it seemed as if Jamie might ignore the question completely, she raised her eyes, held his gaze.

"No, it was never a conscious decision. More like giving up hope. But I've found since I've returned home, family is very important to me. I'd like the chance to have a family of my own."

Ryan glanced away. Disappointment settled heavily in his stomach.

"Ryan, where's this thing with us going?"

Damn. He'd made the opening for this conversation, now he simply had to face it.

Clearing his throat, he said, "I care about you a lot."

"But?"

"But it wouldn't be fair of me promise you something I can't deliver." He ignored the part of him that had come to hope. Instead, he recited the safe, the familiar. "I'm not a family man. Not while I'm racing. Maybe not ever."

Her mouth trembled at the corners, but she quickly covered with a sad smile. "Thank you for being honest."

He didn't have the guts to ask her if she might marry him on those terms. Or even move in with him. She deserved the whole enchilada, kids and all. Not waiting for a vague someday that might never come.

Their conversation after that was stilted as they searched for safe topics.

Ryan couldn't help wondering if it was the beginning of the end. The end of something he'd never asked for, never anticipated and wasn't sure he even wanted. All he knew was he wanted to figure out a way for them to make it as a couple. Because he wasn't sure he could stand watching Jamie walk away.

CHAPTER NINETEEN

AFTER A NIGHT spent tossing and turning, Jamie awoke feeling worn out. The atmosphere seemed dense and damp, even in an air-conditioned hotel room.

She showered quickly, hoping to shake off the fatigue. Afterward, she threw on her Tanner T-shirt and jeans, dried her hair and pulled it back in an elastic band.

Applying blush, lip gloss and mascara, she figured it was an effort to convince Ryan what he'd be missing if he let her go. The thought brought a lump to her throat. Nothing had been said about the future of their relationship.

Her eyes blurred. *Children.* She could envision raising a family with Ryan, even with two demanding careers. Why couldn't he even consider it?

She drove slowly to the track, pondering their predicament. When she arrived, the parking lot was busy already. She found a space, parked and put on the lanyard with her pit pass. She normally would have relished the sights and sounds, the excitement building before a big race. Today, all she could contemplate was *what if.*

Her pulse quickened as she entered the hauler and

saw Ryan discussing stats with Bill. His smile was wide when he glanced up at her.

She waved, small and unsure, then sat on the leather sofa to wait.

A few minutes later, he came over and sat next to her. His gaze was warm. “Hey.”

“Hey.” Jamie felt as if her throat were closing up. It felt good to be sitting close to him, to absorb his scent, feed on the electric excitement, breathe the same air. Too good to waste worrying about the future. And yet, the future wouldn’t seem to let her go.

He grasped her hand, rubbing his thumb over her knuckles. “You okay? You were kinda quiet last night.”

“I was just tired. Had a lot on my mind.”

“Anything I should know about?”

She hesitated, unsure if there was anything to say. Some things were a given. “Not just yet.”

“I’m here if you want to talk.”

Chuckling, she said, “Yeah, like you have anything on your mind but winning that race today.”

“You know me well.” He grew serious. “But I mean it, Jamie. Talk to me.”

“Maybe later.” There was no way she’d lay this on him before a big race.

The room grew still, all conversation stopped.

Jamie glanced up and saw Bill restrain Brent. The kid’s face was red and he hollered something. Then she looked beyond and saw Trey standing in the doorway.

“You’ve got a lot of nerve showing up here after you sold us out. I’m gonna kick your butt.” For the easy-going Brent to fly off the handle demonstrated just how much pressure the team was under. And how betrayed they felt.

"Come on, Brent. You and me'll go outside." Bill herded the boy through the hauler. The room became quiet as everyone seemed to collectively hold their breath.

Everyone, except Ryan. He stood, squaring his shoulders. "You couldn't have picked another time, Trey?"

"Sorry, Ry, I know the timing sucks. Bill said you've been wanting to talk to me and I need you to clear up a misunderstanding. A detective came to my house yesterday. Says I'm 'an investigative lead' in the burglary at your shop. That's bogus and you know it. All it'll take is a phone call from you to clear it up."

Jamie shifted uneasily. "Can't this be handled another time?"

"Not when I could be arrested at any moment. Ryan, I worked my butt off for you. You owe me to at least listen."

"You also left me high and dry." Ryan's jaw set, a sure indication he was trying to retain control of his emotions. "But I can listen."

"That's all I ask."

Ryan raised his voice to address the remaining crew. "I need everyone out while I talk to Trey."

Jamie hesitated. Her instinct was to protect Ryan from distractions on race day. Heck, she'd put her own issues on hold for him.

He glanced at her.

"Please?" His voice was low.

"Okay. I'd do the same in your shoes." Friendships didn't grow on trees. And Ryan had good reason to treasure those he had.

RYAN WAITED for the crew and Jamie to file out. When he heard the door shut, he turned to Trey. "No use standing."

He sat on the leather sofa.

Trey sat at the other end.

"What've you heard around the track about the break-in?" Ryan asked.

Trey frowned. "Not much. I've been staying away from racing. It's…too hard."

Ryan absorbed his statement. He intended to hash out a lot of things with Trey. And the bit about staying away from racing bothered him. Trey was like the rest of the team, including Ryan—eating, sleeping, breathing racing.

"Did the cops mention you were caught on tape entering the shop the night it happened?"

Trey laughed, a sound harsh with disbelief. "I might not have left under the best circumstances, but I'm no thief. You can't really believe I'd do something like that?"

Ryan was grimly satisfied to see hurt flash quickly in his friend's eyes, before it was replaced by anger. He wanted his friend to feel what he'd felt.

"I thought I knew you, Trey. But you up and quit on me without any warning. Now you're ditching racing completely. Makes me wonder if I knew you at all."

"I'm not ditching it completely… Just taking a break while I reevaluate."

"What's to reevaluate?"

"It's…personal."

"This is me you're talking to. We've shared personal stuff before."

Trey ran his hand through his hair. "Because I'm

scared. And embarrassed. And didn't know what else to do."

"What're you scared about?"

"Sheila's pregnant."

"Oh." Ryan didn't know what else to say.

Trey held up his hand. "I know what you're thinking. But we were careful. It's just…one of those things."

"So why'd you quit? You could have come to me and we'd have worked something out."

"Sheila needs me." He hesitated. "I want to marry her and be a family. I can't do that if I'm on the road."

Understanding dawned. Trey was living Ryan's worst nightmare.

"Isn't there another way? Maybe have Sheila travel with you?"

"You know as well as I do how tough it is. We're on the road thirty-six weeks out of the year. She's been having some problems. The doctor says she needs to get her stress level down."

"Wow." He looked at his friend with a whole new respect. And more than a little uneasiness. "You gave it all up for her, for your child?"

Trey nodded. "I'm sorry about the way I left…sorry I didn't come clean with you. I just needed to get my head on straight. I realized I couldn't live with myself if she lost the baby because I was on the road."

"If there's anything I can do…"

"Yeah, well, you can give me that information your mom sent about insurance underwriting school." His grin was crooked, his eyes shadowed.

Ryan repressed a shudder. "Anything but that, man."

"Just a thought. And about the other night, I came by

to get some of my tools. It would have been too hard when everyone was there."

"Probably."

"Ry, I might be a lot of things, but I'm not stupid. I wouldn't look straight at the security camera if I were robbing the place. Remember, I worked with the security company setting up the cameras?"

"I remember. For whatever it's worth, I admire what you're doing. You're a braver man than I am."

"Not brave. Just trying to make the best of things." His friend's defeated tone saddened him.

"You're the best crew chief I ever had. And a good friend, too. If you decide you want to come back, let me know."

"Nope. I'm done with the road. When you're in serious contention for the Cup and sponsors start throwing money around, will you consider me for the shop? It's bare bones now but won't always be."

"You got it, Trey." He stood, clapped his friend on the shoulder. "I'll call that detective and let him know you're not the one they want."

The question was, who *had* torn up his shop?

JAMIE WAITED a few minutes after Trey left before returning inside the hauler. She wanted to give Ryan space to deal with whatever the two former friends had discussed.

"Everything okay?" she asked.

"What? Oh, yeah, fine. I called the detective and told him to lay off Trey."

Jamie hesitated. "So he explained what we saw on the tape?"

"Yes. He wanted to come by at night when no one

was around. Quitting was as hard on him as it was on us. It's not what he wanted."

"They why'd he quit?"

"He wants to make a home with Sheila."

"There's something you're not telling me." Jamie snapped her fingers. "She's pregnant. That's why the heat got to her so bad the other day."

"Shh. Keep it quiet. I don't know if it's common knowledge yet. She's having some problems with the pregnancy and needs him to stay in town."

Her chest ached with need. A baby, a family of her own. Why were children all the more important since she'd met Ryan? Because she'd finally met a man with whom she wanted it all—a home, children, the whole ball of wax.

"Don't look so sad. He'll come back to the series eventually. It's in his blood."

She chuckled at his simplistic view. And opted for honesty. "I'm not sad for him…I'm a little envious."

"The baby stuff?"

"Yes," she murmured, avoiding his gaze. Afraid she'd see irritation.

A part of her hoped he'd rush right in and say he'd changed his mind and wanted babies, too. Instead, he opened his mouth and shut it again while the color drained from his face. Finally, he said, "I thought you understood."

"Ryan, our relationship happened so suddenly. There's no reason to cross this bridge right now."

Yes, there is.

She ignored the warning bells clamoring in her head. There was no need to force a showdown. Ultimatums weren't her style.

Besides, an ultimatum would mean she was willing to risk what they had on a nebulous future.

"Jamie, I owe you the truth. Fatherhood is something I'm not willing to contemplate for a long while. Maybe not ever. There's a good chance I'm not cut out for that type of life."

"Why not?"

"Come on. You know my history. You know what my career means to me. How can you even ask?"

Jamie felt as if he was forcing her to lay her cards on the table. Taking a deep breath, she said, "Because being with you allowed me to dream of things I hadn't considered for a long, long time. Things I'd pretty much given up on ever having. And I want them with you, Ryan."

"You want me to give up my dreams so I can become someone you'll hate? Someone *I'll* hate?"

"I'd never ask you to give up your dreams. I have to believe it's possible to have both. It's not something we need to decide today."

She reached out, hoping he'd let it go. When he didn't move closer, didn't take her hand, she allowed her arm to drop to her side.

"You're wrong. We do have to decide today. Because if we don't, it will only get harder. And someone is going to get hurt even worse. Or you'll get pregnant and we'll end up like Trey and Sheila."

Jamie stared at the man she loved and saw that he truly believed what he said.

"I thought you were braver than that," she whispered.

His shoulders sagged. "You've got it all wrong. This is the only way I can keep my edge and protect you."

"You keep your edge and I'll worry about protecting myself. I'm pretty darn good at it these days." She shook her head. "You know what, I've always accepted what people told me was enough instead of fighting for what my heart said was right. I can't fight for both of us, Ryan. I hope your career keeps you warm at night. I hope the rev of engines is as musical as a baby's laugh. Because we *could* have it all. Settling for anything less is a crock."

Jamie slung her purse over her shoulder. She wanted nothing more than to make a beeline for the airport and board the next plane bound for Arkansas. But she would finish what she started. "If you'll excuse me, I'm going topside."

RYAN TIGHTENED his hands on the wheel.

Darlington. A wicked track under the best of circumstances. He'd have to be on his toes to bring in a win. And he was determined to do it.

Thoughts of Jamie kept creeping in. Their argument kept playing through his mind. How else could he have handled it? It was the kindest thing for both of them.

Then why did he feel like crap?

He tried to scan the roof of the hauler for her, but his restraint system restricted his movement and peripheral vision. He felt like an Egyptian mummy in a sarcophagus. Sweat trickled down his back, his chest, beneath his armpits.

Focus, Pearce, focus.

He reviewed the strategy he'd set with Bill, but knew strategy could be blown two minutes after the green flag was dropped. The outside line was where everyone would be—it was the logical course. But Darlington was so damn narrow, he'd have to take the openings as they came. Or bump and run to create his own.

Jamie's face flashed through his mind just before the green flag dropped. Then instinct and training kicked in and he pushed her out of his mind.

He jostled for position, inches away from other cars. His pulse pounded, adrenaline flowed and he whooped for the sheer joy of it.

Then things got squirrelly and another car almost shoved him into the wall. He managed to keep under control and merely scraped the wall for a few feet. He didn't doubt the car would end up with a Daytona stripe rubbed along the side, where fiberglass met wall.

One of the young hotshots took the lead. Ryan was eager to chase him down and show him who was boss.

"Hold it steady," Bill said over the radio. "You'll have your shot at him later."

He grinned. His new crew chief knew him well. "Sure thing."

He settled in and held his line, keeping a close eye on the action around him, his movements controlled and smooth. It wouldn't take much at this narrow track to end up in a huge pileup.

The rear of the car slid a bit as he went into Turn Three.

"We're loose, Bill. The tires ought to grab better."

"Yeah, before they disintegrate." Darlington was notoriously hard on tires.

His spotter came on the air, warning of debris on the track. It was starting already. Steering around hunks of rubber, he hoped none of it would fly up and wedge in the oil pump belt like what happened to one of his competitors last year.

The spotter advised Ryan of a wreck behind him and told him the best way to maneuver around on the yellow flag.

"Too early to take tires, Ryan. Want to conserve that rubber if you can. Need to pit for a tighter setup?"

"No, I'll run it for now."

A few minutes later, he wished he'd stopped. The guy behind him started to pass, but Ryan held him off. Until the Number 63 car got loose in the turn, scraped the wall and things got crazy.

CHAPTER TWENTY

JAMIE FELT as if her heart was in her throat. She clenched her hands and half rose from her lawn chair atop the hauler.

"Come on, Ryan," she murmured, half prayer, half command.

The Number 63 car swerved, threatening to do a one-eighty. But Ryan got it under control.

She released her breath. How did the wives and girlfriends do this, week in and week out? They had to be the bravest women alive.

Sadness washed over her because she would never know if she was up to the challenge. But she would still be an independent engine builder, her life's ambition. Just not someone special in Ryan's heart.

Jamie watched the rest of the race through a haze. She was vaguely aware that the motor she'd built was doing great. If only the crew could manage the suspension and tires....

It seemed like only moments later when she realized they were down to the last fifty laps. Things were going to get wild.

Sure enough, Ryan made his bid for first place. He passed the second and third place cars but couldn't quite catch the leader.

Then it was the last pit stop and Ryan took four tires. Jamie nodded. He'd lose a few seconds, but with the loose handling, the new tires were essential.

Sure enough, he made up the lost time almost immediately.

They were down to the last five laps when the lead car approached the tail runners, who didn't want to be lapped. None of them were giving way. It gave Ryan the chance he needed. When the lead car went around, Ryan shot through behind him, going high, passing him on the outside. One lap to go. All he needed to do was hold the lead.

The checkered flag came down—as Ryan passed the finish line.

Jumping to her feet, Jamie cheered for Ryan and the team—men who'd grown to be a part of her life in such a short time. Then she forced herself to do what needed to be done. She climbed down the steps of the hauler, walked through the gate and found her car. The sound of Ryan's engine revving while he did victory doughnuts made her smile. When she brushed her hand across her cheek, Jamie found she'd been smiling through her tears.

RYAN WAITED for the commercial break to end before he peeled back the window net and hauled himself out the window.

The bursts of light were blinding as photo after photo was shot. He kept smiling, changing hats, accepting sponsored beverages and thanking the fans and his sponsors. When his sight cleared, he glanced around for Jamie.

And, when he'd thanked all the requisite people, he told the reporters what a terrific job Tanner Motors had done on his engine.

"Ms. Jamie Tanner is the technician and she deserves to come take a bow. Jamie, where are you?" He glanced around, but didn't see her beautiful face.

There was a murmur as someone approached from the back of the crowd. The green Tanner T-shirt and hat were familiar, but disappointing.

Ryan swallowed the lump in his throat but recovered quickly. "And here's Tom Tanner of Tanner Performance Motors. Thanks for pulling my rear from the fire with such a fantastic engine."

"Our pleasure." Tom nodded and smiled. His smile didn't quite reach his eyes.

JAMIE SWORE around the pencil clutched in her teeth as she worked on the computer, projecting the budgetary needs of her department for the coming fiscal year—her attempt to go above and beyond for the good of the business. This part of the job really sucked.

"I heard that. Mom will wash your mouth out with soap."

She saved her document and removed the pencil from her mouth. "How do you do all this paperwork?"

Tom shrugged. "It's not that bad once you get used to it. Though I'd much rather be out in the field drumming up business."

"Not in the engine shop?"

"Funny you should mention that. I've found I don't miss it as much as I thought I would. Must be a case of the shop being the last cookie in the jar."

Jamie raised an eyebrow. "What?"

"It was so much more attractive because I knew you wanted it. The thrill of competition. Now I'm thinking maybe there are enough cookies to go around."

His admission made her smile, almost chasing away the ache of missing Ryan. "You know what, Tom? It takes a big man to admit that. I think you might grow up to be a decent human being someday."

"Thanks for the vote of confidence." He leaned against the door-frame. "You see the race yesterday?"

She nodded, unable to speak.

"Another win for Pearce."

"Yeah."

"That motor you built is fantastic. I'm impressed, Sis."

Jamie held up her hand. "Please, stop the compliments. I might start thinking you want something."

Guilt flashed across his face before he composed a bland expression.

"Out with it. What do you want?"

"Call it brotherly interest. What do you intend to do about Ryan?"

"I don't intend to do anything. It didn't work out. End of story."

"Mind if I ask why it didn't work?"

"Yes, I mind. I didn't ask you why it didn't work out with Mindy, Cindy, Chelsea and Brittany one, two and three, did I?"

"Ouch. No need to go for the jugular." He moved to the chair across from her desk and sat. "This brotherly concern stuff is hard for me. I'm still feeling my way along."

"You know, a little bit of that concern can go a long way. Especially when it involves my failed love life."

"Did you even tell the guy why you walked out on him?"

Jamie glared at him. She so didn't want to be having this conversation. It felt as if her heart was being stomped to bits. "Yes. I called him later that night and explained we wanted different things. He…understood. He'd actually made the same point in a roundabout way earlier in the day."

Tom patted her hand. "I'm sorry. It's really crummy. I thought you two were really gonna make it."

Her eyes blurred. She blinked back the moisture and forced a smile. "Thanks, Tom. You're not bad for a kid brother."

"You're not so bad yourself. You deserve to be happy. When I saw you with Pearce and realized my very self-contained sister had fallen head-over-heels in love, I thought maybe you didn't know what you were doing. But then I saw Pearce couldn't seem to take his eyes off you. How much he wanted you to be there with him in Victory Lane. I understood. I thought you had a connection like Mom and Dad have."

Her heart ached anew. Her voice was husky when she said, "I thought so, too. But it wasn't meant to be."

"You're sure? Because it looked to me like you could be the one to carry on Mom and Dad's legacy of a tight marriage."

"He doesn't want marriage or children, Tom." Her voice grew husky. "Ever."

His eyes widened. "Now I think I see. Who does he think he is, messing with my sister?" His outrage might have been comical if it hadn't been so sweet.

"It's not like that. He was…very good to me." Jamie

squared her shoulders, trying to appear strong and in control. Her quivering lower lip refused to cooperate. "It's just one of those things. An insurmountable roadblock."

He rubbed his thumb across her cheek. "Aw, don't cry."

Jamie went around the desk and walked into his open arms. He patted her back while she cried. A few moments later, she sniffed. "You know something, I don't know what I did without you for so long."

He winced. "Better reserve judgment till you hear what I have to offer."

Jamie dabbed at her eyes with the hem of her T-shirt.

Tom sighed, withdrawing a crisp white handkerchief from his pocket and handed it to her. "It's amazing we come from the same family."

She smiled and blew her nose. "Yeah, but it works somehow, you know?"

He grinned and punched her in the shoulder. "I know. The questions is whether you're willing to put your money where your mouth is."

"What's that supposed to mean?"

"Dad wants to come back part-time when the doctor releases him. Mom's driving him nuts. You know he'll want to retain control of the shop. With the expansion, we can't pay someone to come in full time. Would you consider coming in full-time at half-salary, with a deferred bonus?"

She narrowed her eyes. "What will you be doing?"

"Marketing, sales and customer service. And we'll promote one of the clerks to office manager to take on more of the administrative responsibility. That way, neither you nor I have to mess with it."

Hallelujah! Work with her dad in the shop and not have loads of paperwork? It was darn near ideal. Except for the money thing. Fortunately, her severance package from the automaker had been generous.

But there was no need to let Tom think he was in control. "Let's have lunch and discuss those deferred bonuses. And of course I'd want everything in writing. Especially the part where I take over the shop when Dad retires."

"You must've heard wrong. There *isn't* a part like that."

"There is now." Jamie looped her arm through his and they walked out the door arm in arm.

It was good to be home.

TOM FIDGETED in the passenger seat, his stomach sinking as they pulled into their parents' drive. "I don't like being shanghai'd, Jamie. I gave you everything you wanted. Can't you be happy with that?"

Jamie glanced at him, turning off the ignition. "Nobody gave me anything. I've *earned* my place at Tanner."

He grumbled, but didn't belabor the point. "Why are we here?"

"I want to make sure everyone is on the same page before you have the documents drawn up. Dad still outranks you. And Mom has veto power the President would envy."

He followed her up the walkway, waiting as she rang the bell. His collar suddenly seemed tight. Loosening his tie, he unbuttoned the top button.

"Jamie Lynn, Tom, what a nice surprise." Their

mother hugged them both in turn. "Come in. You didn't need to knock, you know."

"Hey, we didn't want to interrupt something. I told Jamie it wasn't a good—"

"Nonsense. Your father will be delighted to see you." She turned and they followed her through the door.

"Jimmy," she called. "The kids are here."

They found him in his recliner. He yawned, pushing down the foot rest and sitting up. "Must've dozed off."

"Sweet tea, anyone?" Susan asked.

"No, we won't be staying long, will we, Sis?"

Jamie fiddled with the strap on her purse. "No, it won't take long at all. Mom, Daddy, I wanted you to be aware of the terms Tom and I have agreed on."

"Terms about what, dear?"

"My permanent position at Tanner." She went on to describe the agreement. "And I'll be President of Technical Services when Daddy retires."

Their dad didn't say anything. He exchanged a glance with their mother and waited.

She said, "Jamie, you know we love having you back in town. But I, I mean we, have reservations about you taking on that kind of position."

Tom watched the pain flash in Jamie's eyes. Suddenly, he realized how difficult it must have been for her. Once he'd made the effort to keep an open mind, he'd understood how incredibly talented she was. And admired how hard she'd worked without expecting anything in return.

He stepped forward, but Jamie held up her hand to forestall him.

"Your points are valid, Mom. I'm sure you're aware I had a relationship with a driver. And yes, a career got in the way. But it was his, not mine. The outcome would have been the same no matter what my job had been."

Their mother patted Jamie's arm. "It's broken my heart to see you so sad. But you've been brave and moved on."

"My job is one of the things that's allowed me to move on. I love everything about my position at Tanner. And I can't think of anything more fulfilling than working alongside Daddy when he comes back."

Their dad made a sound low in his throat. His eyes were suspiciously bright. But he didn't step in. This was between Jamie and Mom. Always had been, always would be.

"All I've ever wanted was for you to be happy. I may never understand why you love engines so much. But, as you pointed out before, it's legal and it makes you happy. Are you positive this is what you want?"

Jamie placed her hand over Susan's. Her voice was gentle when she said, "Yes. Your approval would mean a lot, Mom."

Tom bit back a smile. His throat got scratchy.

Their mother was silent for what seemed to be an eternity. He wasn't sure if she was processing Jamie's statement or hoping she would retract it.

Finally, she glanced at their father.

He nodded slowly.

Mom turned, her eyes moist, enfolding Jamie in a hug. "Then of course you have my blessing, dear."

RYAN SAT in the hauler and soaked up the air conditioning.

The place was deserted while everyone went about their various duties. A pang of loneliness hit him square in the chest. He wondered what Jamie was doing. Wondered if she'd thought about him in the past two weeks. He'd certainly thought about her. Sometimes it seemed as if he couldn't get the woman off his mind.

"You're a damn fool." Bill placed a soda on the table and sat in the chair next to him.

Ryan intentionally misunderstood. "I'm driving nearly perfectly."

"It's not your driving I'm talking about. You let Jamie get away, but you're too stubborn to tell her you were wrong and beg her to work it out."

"I'm not wrong. That's the problem. I'm not cut out for family life. We'd both end up miserable."

Bill nodded. "Sometimes, sure. It goes with the territory. But you'd also have times so good you thought you'd died and gone to heaven."

Ryan raised an eyebrow. "Was it that way for you?"

"Yep. Until I screwed up."

"My point exactly. This my lifestyle, my genes. They're a recipe for disaster. I'm bound to screw up big time."

"Maybe. But some guys manage to have it all. How come them and not you?"

"They don't have my legacy, Bill."

"You're right there, son. Some have a lot worse." He stood, his voice gruff. "I never thought I'd see you take the coward's way out. Quit your moping if you don't intend to do anything about it."

Ryan's shoulders sagged as the closest person he had to a father stalked out of the hauler.

JAMIE SWITCHED on the fluorescent lights and inhaled the familiar aroma of motor oil and solvent. This garage would be hers someday. And until then, she had the opportunity of a lifetime to train with Daddy, learn more of the subtleties of the trade. And make up for the lost time she'd spent away from him. His heart attack had made her realize he wouldn't be around forever. The thought saddened her.

Jamie only hoped spending time with her family would fill the ache inside. Funny, she'd finally achieved her dream, but couldn't seem to find her enthusiasm.

A strand of hair swung in her eyes. She reached into her top desk drawer for an elastic band. Her fingers curved around a small plastic bag.

She withdrew the O-rings from Ryan's carburetor. She'd meant to do more research, but hadn't had time. Just as she'd intended to call the insurance agent and find out if their liability coverage applied to situations like this. Slowly closing the drawer, she forgot about tying back her hair.

Removing the rings from the bag, she frowned. They should have been pliable rubber washers. Instead, they were brittle. No wonder the carburetor had failed. And by visual inspection, they appeared to be passenger grade parts.

"You've put in a lot of hours lately."

Jamie started, placing the bag in her back pocket. For some reason, it was important to keep it secret. For now.

"So have you, Hal. Everything okay?"

"Yep. Just getting caught up on paperwork."

"Have we had any complaints about carburetors recently?"

"No. Why?"

"Just wondering. I need to print up some stats and then I'm outta here. Oh, by the way, have you seen that fuel pump Pearce sent?"

He rubbed the back of his neck. "Can't say that I have."

"I thought I put it in the locked bin, but it's not there."

"Hmm. Don't know." He glanced away. "But I'll be on the lookout for it."

"Thanks, Hal. Have a good weekend."

He nodded. "See ya."

She printed up the Pearce account and cross referenced the list of suppliers. She'd go over it at her apartment. Nothing better to do this weekend. And she had no intention of watching the NASCAR NEXTEL Cup race on TV. That would be too painful.

RYAN WANDERED through the impromptu infield city where the drivers and their families set up their home-away-from-home for the weekend. Top-of-the-line motor homes resided next to a few modest models like Ryan's.

Today, there seemed to be kids everywhere. Or maybe he was just more aware of them.

Ryan smothered a smile as he nodded to a driver sitting beneath the canopy of his motor home. Aaron Tate teetered on a pint-size chair, holding a tiny tea cup, pinkie extended. Two girls about five years old giggled at his ineptitude.

"No, Daddy, you *sip* the tea."

"Sure, sweetheart."

The fact that the guy could run with the best at one hundred and eighty miles per hour apparently didn't qualify him for tea drinking.

"Hey, Pearce, this is our secret," the driver called.

"Sure it is."

He grinned and walked on, seeing little details that suddenly took on more significance. Families holding barbecues, guys attending to honey-do projects, the sound of yappy dogs and bickering couples. It was probably no different from most neighborhoods on a Saturday afternoon.

Bill's comments really irritated him. The man had called him a coward. He wasn't, was he?

Ryan veered off the path to avoid a game of catch. The boy appeared to be about eight. When Ryan turned to look over his shoulder, he realized the father was a hard-nosed driver who wouldn't give an inch on the track. Yet he encouraged the boy, even when the child's throws went wild.

"Good try, son."

An ache of loss hit Ryan so unexpectedly he almost stopped in his tracks. He remembered all the times he'd longed to share ordinary moments like these with his father.

Glancing back, he noted the easy relationship between father and son. Somehow he knew that didn't happen overnight. It was the result of consistent sacrifices and love. Balancing what was best for the family with the realities of life on the road. Ted Emory had made it work. He hadn't left just because his kid asked for a few minutes of his time.

But the guy didn't have the Pearce family legacy.

No, his was worse.

Ryan stopped, stunned. Ted had been very open about his past and the struggles he'd had coming up.

Ryan had heard him speak about the way his father had let him down, time after time. And yet, he'd gotten past that. He now worked his butt off to do things differently with his own son. It was a *choice*.

The thought was so simple, yet so astounding, it made his head ache. Maybe Ryan's father had been a crummy dad because that's what he'd chosen. He'd never cared about anyone but himself. Maybe Ryan could choose differently for himself, just as Ted Emory and Aaron Tate had done.

CHAPTER TWENTY-ONE

JAMIE WISHED she could be anywhere else at the moment. The break room at Tanner doubled as the conference room. She gathered the newspapers from the table and threw them in the recycling bin.

Tom entered, carrying a to-go cup of soda. "You sure you want to handle this?"

"Yes. It's my responsibility."

"Technically it's Dad's mess that was handed to you."

"Nobody feels worse about it than Dad. He wanted to be here, but I suggested he call Hal later if he felt it was important. If this gets ugly, I don't want Dad exposed to the stress firsthand."

Tom shook his head. "I never would have guessed. Hal's been here forever."

"I wouldn't have thought so, either, except the evidence was pretty persuasive."

Hal entered the room. His gaze darted from Tom to Jamie. "You wanted to see me?"

"Yes. Have a seat." Jamie closed the door behind him.

"My review's not for another couple months..."

"I wish this were as simple as a review." She placed a file folder in front of him. "I'd like you to look at these and explain what happened."

The color drained from his face as he opened the file. He swallowed hard. "Looks like purchase orders and delivery manifests."

"And inventory reports. Is that your signature acknowledging receipt on the manifests?"

"You know it is."

"It looks like we've been paying for a lot of parts we never received."

Hal half stood. "Now wait a minute—"

"Why, Hal?" She suddenly felt very tired. "You've worked for us for nearly twenty years."

"I didn't do anything."

"At the very least you got a kickback for all those parts we never received. Or ordered them and sold them black market."

"Why would I do something like that?" his voice was an octave too high.

"That's what I want to know. I'd also like to know about the Pearce carburetor and fuel pump. They were junk on the inside, weren't they? Rebuilt from tired old parts and painted up to look new. That's why they conveniently went missing."

"You're crazy."

"Far from it," Tom interjected. "I'd suggest you come clean."

Jamie crossed her arms over her chest. "This really put Tanner Motors in a bad position. We've had to eat the costs on both Pearce engines to make it right. Worse, we don't know if insurance will cover it. Come clean and we might consider letting you off with repaying our parts costs for the engines. Otherwise, we go to the police."

Hal's eyes widened. "I can't go to jail—the twins are less than a year old. They were preemies and we've had a lot of medical expenses."

Glancing at Tom, Jamie wondered what she should do. Sending the man to jail might not be best for anyone.

She sat down. "Is that why you did it?"

He nodded. "First it was the infertility treatments. Then Tracy quit her job because the twins needed special care…"

"Why didn't you go to my father? Sometimes he'll work out a loan for situations like these."

"He'd already loaned me five thousand dollars. And the other employees took up a collection. I couldn't ask for more."

"So you stole instead? And put drivers at risk?"

Hanging his head, he said, "I was gonna pay him back. I'll resign immediately."

"I understand you were under a lot of pressure, but that's no excuse." Jamie slid a pad of paper across the table. "I want you to note every single inferior part and the engines they were installed in. If you do that, we won't go to the police. We'll set up a repayment schedule. It doesn't have to be a lot at first, but enough to show you're genuinely trying."

He nodded, his resemblance to a turkey more pronounced.

When he finished the list, she was grateful to see they only had one motor to pull. The rest were still on-site at Tanner.

After Hal left, she said, "It could have been much worse."

"Good thing you caught it, Sis."

"I only wish Ryan's career didn't take a hit because of it." She sighed. "You might want to meet with our attorney and see if there's any restitution we should make to the Pearce Team beyond what we've already done."

"Like maybe giving the guy a second chance?"

"He doesn't want a second chance." And that was perhaps the part that hurt the most.

JAMIE'S FATHER opened the door. "Hi, Kitten, thanks for coming."

"I'm glad you called." She hugged him and stepped inside. "You said Mom went shopping?"

"Yeah, it just didn't seem right, being by myself, even though the doc said it would be okay."

"Hey, I'm always glad to have an excuse to hang out with you."

He returned to his recliner. "Do you want something to drink? A soda?"

"No, I'm fine."

The professor and Mr. Howell droned in the background.

Clearing his throat, he said, "I kind of asked you here on false pretenses."

"Oh?"

"I've had a lot of time to think about things lately and I need to apologize.... When you were a little girl, I liked having you as my sidekick. Then you got to be a teen and still could turn wrenches better than most men. And I still liked having you be my sidekick."

"Thanks, Daddy."

"I knew it was in your blood. I thought your mom

would eventually see that. But the older you got, the more insistent she got that you do other things. The Poultry Princess title is an example. She loves you, Kitten, and only wanted what she thought was best for you. I knew she was wrong though. Instead of standing my ground, I gave in to keep the peace. I'm sorry."

Jamie cleared her throat. "It means a lot to hear you say that."

He nodded. "I just thought you should know."

They watched TV for a few minutes, the lack of conversation strained.

"Daddy?"

"Yes?"

"Would you do the same thing all over again?"

"God help me, Kitten, I'm not sure what I would do. It's a terrible thing to be torn between the people you love. But I made a vow to your mother when I married her. I figured if I kept my vows and honored her above all others, including you and your brother, you children would benefit in the end."

"You did the best you could, Daddy." The realization freed some of the bitterness lodged in her throat. "I don't agree with how you handled it, but I…understand."

"You're a good girl. And one heck of a technician, too. I'm proud of you, Jamie Lynn."

Jamie blinked away tears. She reached over and grasped his callused hand. "I'm glad."

Conversation lagged as the professor came up with another brilliant idea for escaping the island.

"Are you happy?"

The question caught her by surprise. "Sure, I guess."

"What happened with Pearce? I thought you'd fallen for the guy."

She chuckled hollowly. "I did. It didn't work out."

"How come?"

This was the most intimate conversation she could remember having with her dad. She almost longed for the relative safety of a racing debate. "I'm starting to understand how important family is. Ryan's not a family kind of guy."

"Most men aren't. Or don't think they are. I certainly wasn't."

"You always said it was love at first sight with Mom."

"It was. Doesn't mean I didn't fight it all the way."

"It's different with Ryan. He didn't have a very good role model growing up." Not like she'd had. There was never any doubt that her parents loved each other.

"A man who drives like he does has to be pretty smart. He'll figure it out."

"I wish it were true."

"When you came back home after my heart attack, I noticed changes in you. You were ready to fight for what you wanted. So, how come you gave up Pearce without a fight?"

"I was scared, Daddy." The statement was wrenched from her without time for denial.

"Sure, we're all scared where love's concerned."

"What scares me the most is the thought of really trying and have it not work in the end."

"So if you were a driver, you'd stay at the back of the pack because it wouldn't hurt so much if you crashed?"

"Crashes can happen no matter where you are on the track. So I have the choice of sitting out or using every bit of knowledge and skill I have to win."

Her dad nodded slowly. "That's the way I see it."

"In the past, I've allowed other people to control the choices I made. You, Mom, Tom. This time I came back prepared to fight for what I wanted. You're saying that if I fight for Ryan and lose, at least I'll know I tried my best."

He held her gaze. "You won't lose, Kitten. You are your mother's daughter."

Jamie went to her father and kissed him on the cheek. "Thank you, Daddy."

"YOU'RE A COWARD, Ryan Pearce."

Ryan bumped his head on the hood as he straightened, cursing under his breath.

He turned to see Jamie standing in the garage doorway. His mood instantly brightened. Then he remembered he shouldn't be so happy to see her. Jamie's presence shouldn't make that big a difference in his outlook.

But it did.

He wiped his hands on a shop cloth. "What're you doing here?"

"I came to see you. A wise man pointed out the pitfalls of playing it safe."

"There are times when caution is a good thing."

She propped her hands on her hips. "This coming from a man who drives one hundred and eighty miles an hour? Caution is like anything else, there can be too much of a good thing. You can get so cautious you take yourself out of the race. Life isn't meant to come in neat little boxes where you separate all the stuff that's uncomfortable or messy."

"If it were, you certainly wouldn't be here." Ryan couldn't help but grin. Damn, it was good to see her. He stepped closer. His voice was husky when he asked, "How've you been, Jamie?"

"Not so good. I had to fire Hal." She explained about Hal's dishonesty. "Here this man was risking it all for his family. And you and I are risking nothing so you can avoid having a family."

He tried to follow her logic. He didn't like where it was headed. "I'm not avoiding anything. I made a choice."

"What about me? Don't I get a say in it?" Jamie came closer, holding his gaze. "I've made some mistakes in my life. The biggest was backing away from a fight and just accepting what everyone decided could be mine. I'm not doing that now. I love you, Ryan, and I think you love me."

Her words started an ache in his gut. Not because they were untrue, but because he had the feeling Jamie expected him to be courageous.

"Am I wrong?" she asked.

"It's not that simple, and you know it."

"It can be."

"How?"

"We take a chance, give it all we've got. Have faith that we can make it work."

"I don't know how to be a husband."

"I don't know how to be a wife. But I'm willing to learn. Some of it will be trial and error—you've got to admit there are aspects that will be fun to practice." Mischief glinted in her eyes.

He reached for her, but stopped himself. "And what if I screw up big time? What if I'm not cut out for family life?"

"That's a chance I'm willing to take. Question is, do you have the courage to give it a try?"

"But you want kids."

She sighed, as if disappointed at his denseness. "Yes, I do. But I'm willing to wait a few years. If that ship has sailed by then, we might adopt." She touched his arm. "See, I'm already learning compromise. How about you?"

He wrapped his arms around her, pulling her to his chest, as if he could make things turn out right if he held onto her tightly enough. His vision blurred. "Aw, Jamie, I've missed you so much it hurt. I went to call you a bunch of times. But, I…"

She gazed up at him, touching his cheek. "I'm scared, too. Terrified that you'll turn me away. Please don't do that."

"I'll never do that. If you're willing to take the chance, so am I."

"I love you, Ryan. We'll make it work."

The certainty in her voice made him smile. "Yes, we will. I love you, too, Jamie. You're already in my heart. I want you in my home, my bed, my garage. Forever.

* * * * *

Mediterranean Nights

Join the guests and crew of Alexandra's Dream, *the newest luxury ship to set sail on the romantic Mediterranean, as they experience the glamorous world of cruising.*

A new Harlequin continuity series
begins in June 2007 with
FROM RUSSIA, WITH LOVE
by Ingrid Weaver

Marina Artamova books a cabin on the luxurious cruise ship Alexandra's Dream, *when she finds out that her orphaned nephew and his adoptive father are aboard. She's determined to be reunited with the boy...but the romantic ambience of the ship and her undeniable attraction to a man she considers her enemy are about to interfere with her quest!*

Turn the page for a sneak preview!

Piraeus, Greece

"THERE SHE IS, Stefan. *Alexandra's Dream*." David Anderson squatted beside his new son and pointed at the dark blue hull that towered above the pier. The cruise ship was a majestic sight, twelve decks high and as long as a city block. A circle of silver and gold stars, the logo of the Liberty Cruise Line, gleamed from the swept-back smokestack. Like some legendary sea creature born for the water, the ship emanated power from every sleek curve—even at rest it held the promise of motion. "That's going to be our home for the next ten days."

The child beside him remained silent, his cheeks working in and out as he sucked furiously on his thumb. Hair so blond it appeared white ruffled against his forehead in the harbor breeze. The baby-sweet scent unique to the very young mingled with the tang of the sea.

"Ship," David said. "Uh, *parakhod*."

From beneath his bangs, Stefan looked at the *Alexandra's Dream*. Although he didn't release his thumb, the corners of his mouth tightened with the beginning of a smile.

David grinned. That was Stefan's first smile this afternoon, one of only two since they had left the orphanage yesterday. It was probably because of the boat—according to the orphanage staff, the boy loved boats, which was the main reason David had decided to book this cruise. Then again, there was a strong possibility the smile could have been a reaction to David's attempt at pocket-dictionary Russian. Whatever the cause, it was a good start.

The liaison from the adoption agency had claimed that Stefan had been taught some English, but David had yet to see evidence of it. David continued to speak, positive his son would understand his tone even if he couldn't grasp the words. "This is her maiden voyage. Her first trip, just like this is our first trip, and that makes it special." He motioned toward the stage that had been set up on the pier beneath the ship's bow. "That's why everyone's celebrating."

The ship's official christening ceremony had been held the day before and had been a closed affair, with only the cruise-line executives and VIP guests invited, but the stage hadn't yet been disassembled. Banners bearing the blue and white of the Greek flag of the ship's owner, as well as the Liberty circle of stars logo, draped the edges of the platform. In the center, a group of musicians and a dance troupe dressed in traditional white folk costumes performed for the benefit of the *Alexandra's Dream*'s first passengers. Their audience was in a festive mood, snapping their fingers in time to the music while the dancers twirled and wove through their steps.

David bobbed his head to the rhythm of the mandolins. They were playing a folk tune that seemed vaguely familiar, possibly from a movie he'd seen. He hummed a few notes. "Catchy melody, isn't it?"

Stefan turned his gaze on David. His eyes were a striking shade of blue, as cool and pale as a winter horizon and far too solemn for a child not yet five. Still, the smile that hovered at the corners of his mouth persisted. He moved his head with the music, mirroring David's motion.

David gave a silent cheer at the interaction. Hopefully, this cruise would provide countless opportunities for more. "Hey, good for you," he said. "Do you like the music?"

The child's eyes sparked. He withdrew his thumb with a pop. *"Moozika!"*

"Music. Right!" David held out his hand. "Come on, let's go closer so we can watch the dancers."

Stefan grasped David's hand quickly, as if he feared it would be withdrawn. In an instant his budding smile was replaced by a look close to panic.

Did he remember the car accident that had killed his parents? It would be a mercy if he didn't. As far as David knew, Stefan had never spoken of it to anyone. Whatever he had seen had made him run so far from the crash that the police hadn't found him until the next day. The event had traumatized him to the extent that he hadn't uttered a word until his fifth week at the orphanage. Even now he seldom talked.

David sat back on his heels and brushed the hair from Stefan's forehead. That solemn, too-old gaze locked with his, and for an instant, David felt as if he looked back in time at an image of himself thirty years ago.

He didn't need to speak the same language to understand exactly how this boy felt. He knew what it meant to be alone and powerless among strangers, trying to be brave and tough but wishing with every fiber of his being for a place to belong, to be safe, and most of all for someone to love him....

He knew in his heart he would be a good parent to Stefan. It was why he had never considered halting the adoption process after Ellie had left him. He hadn't balked when he'd learned of the recent claim by Stefan's spinster aunt, either; the absentee relative had shown up too late for her case to be considered. The adoption was meant to be. He and this child already shared a bond that went deeper than paperwork or legalities.

A seagull screeched overhead, making Stefan start and press closer to David.

"That's my boy," David murmured. He swallowed hard, struck by the simple truth of what he had just said.

That's my *boy.*

"I CAN'T BE PATIENT, RUDOLPH. I'm not going to stand by and watch my nephew get ripped from his country and his roots to live on the other side of the world."

Rudolph hissed out a slow breath. "Marina, I don't like the sound of that. What are you planning?"

"I'm going to talk some sense into this American kidnapper."

"No. Absolutely not. No offence, but diplomacy is not your strong suit."

"Diplomacy be damned. Their ship's due to sail at five o'clock."

"Then you wouldn't have an opportunity to speak with him even if his lawyer agreed to a meeting."

"I'll have ten days of opportunities, Rudolph, since I plan to be on board that ship."

* * * * *

Follow Marina and David as they join forces to uncover the reason behind little Stefan's unusual silence, and the secret behind the death of his parents....

Look for From Russia, With Love
by Ingrid Weaver
in stores June 2007.